James Sully

Children's Ways

being selections from the author's

James Sully

Children's Ways
being selections from the author's

ISBN/EAN: 9783337276782

Printed in Europe, USA, Canada, Australia, Japan

Cover: Foto ©Andreas Hilbeck / pixelio.de

More available books at **www.hansebooks.com**

CHILDREN'S WAYS

BEING SELECTIONS FROM THE AUTHOR'S
"STUDIES OF CHILDHOOD,"
WITH SOME ADDITIONAL MATTER

BY

JAMES SULLY, M. A., LL. D.

GROTE PROFESSOR OF PHILOSOPHY OF MIND AND LOGIC,
UNIVERSITY COLLEGE, LONDON

AUTHOR OF OUTLINES OF PSYCHOLOGY,
STUDIES OF CHILDHOOD, ETC.

NEW YORK
D. APPLETON AND COMPANY
1897

PREFACE.

THE kindly welcome accorded by the press to my volume *Studies of Childhood* has suggested to me that there was much in it which might be made attractive to a wider class of readers than that addressed in a psychological work. I have, accordingly, prepared the following selections, cutting out abstruse discussions, dropping as far as possible technical language, and adapting the style to the requirements of the general reader. In order to shorten the work the last two chapters—" Extracts from a Father's Diary " and "George Sand's Childhood "—have been omitted. The order of treatment has been altered somewhat, and a number of stories has been added. I hope that the result may succeed in recommending what has long been to myself one of the most delightful of subjects to many who would not be disposed to read a larger and more difficult work, and to draw on a few of these, at least, to a closer and more serious inspection of it.

CONTENTS.

PART I.—AT PLAY.

CHAPTER   PAGE

I. THE REALM OF FANCY : 1
    THE TRANSFORMING WAND 2
    FANCY'S RESTING-PLACES. 6
    IN STORYLAND 8
II. THE ENCHANTMENT OF PLAY. 13
    THE YOUNG PRETENDER 13
    MYSTERIES OF DOLLDOM 18
    SERIOUS SIDE OF PLAY 25

PART II.—AT WORK.

III. ATTACKING OUR LANGUAGE 29
    THE NAMER OF THINGS 30
    THE SENTENCE-BUILDER 33
    THE INTERPRETER OF WORDS 36
IV. THE SERIOUS SEARCHER 40
    THE THOUGHTFUL OBSERVER 40
    THE PERTINACIOUS QUESTIONER 44
V. FIRST THOUGHTS : (a) THE NATURAL WORLD . . 54
    THE FASHION OF THINGS 54
    THE BIGGER WORLD 58
    DREAMS 61
    BIRTH AND GROWTH 64
VI. FIRST THOUGHTS : (b) SELF AND OTHER MYSTERIES . 68
    THE VISIBLE SELF 68
    THE HIDDEN SELF 72
    THE UNREACHABLE PAST 73
    THE SUPERNATURAL WORLD 76
    THE GREAT MAKER 78

CHAPTER		PAGE
VII.	THE BATTLE WITH FEARS: (a) THE ONSLAUGHT	85
	THE BATTERY OF SOUNDS	87
	THE ALARMED SENTINEL	90
VIII.	THE BATTLE WITH FEARS (Continued)	97
	THE ASSAULT OF THE BEASTS	97
	THE NIGHT ATTACK	100
	(b) DAMAGE OF THE ONSLAUGHT	104
	(c) RECOVERY FROM THE ONSLAUGHT	108
IX.	GOOD AND BAD IN THE MAKING	112
	TRACES OF THE BRUTE	112
	THE PROMISE OF HUMANITY	119
	THE LAPSE INTO LYING	124
	FEALTY TO TRUTH	131
X.	REBEL AND SUBJECT	135
	(a) THE STRUGGLE WITH LAW: FIRST TUSSLE WITH AUTHORITY	135
	EVADING THE LAW	137
	THE PLEA FOR LIBERTY	140
	(b) ON THE SIDE OF LAW	142
	THE YOUNG STICKLER FOR THE PROPRIETIES	143
	THE ENFORCER OF RULES	145
XI.	AT THE GATE OF THE TEMPLE	151
	THE GREETING OF BEAUTY	151
	FIRST PEEP INTO THE ART-WORLD	156
	FIRST VENTURES IN CREATION	161
XII.	FIRST PENCILLINGS	171
	THE HUMAN FACE DIVINE	174
	THE VILE BODY	177
	SIDE VIEWS OF THINGS	184

CHILDREN'S WAYS.

PART I.

AT PLAY.

CHAPTER I.

THE REALM OF FANCY.

ONE of the few things we seemed to be certain of with respect to child-nature was that it is fancy-full. Childhood, we all know, is the age for dreaming; for living a life of happy make-believe. Even here, however, we want more accurate observation. For one thing, the play of infantile imagination is probably much less uniform than is supposed. There seem to be very serious children who rarely, if ever, indulge in a wild fancy. Mr. Ruskin has recently told us that when a child he was incapable of acting a part or telling a tale, that he never knew a child "whose thirst for visible fact was at once so eager and so methodic".

One may, nevertheless, safely say that a large majority of the little people are, for a time at least, fancy-bound. A child that did not want to play and cared nothing for the marvels of storyland would surely be regarded as queer and not just what a child ought to be.

Supposing that this is the correct view, there still remains the question whether children's imagination always plays in the same fashion. Now science is beginning to bring to light differences of childish fancy. For one thing it suggests that children have their favourite type of mental imagery, that one child's fancy may habitually move in a coloured world, another in a world of sounds, and so forth. The fascination of *Robinson Crusoe* to many a boy lies in the wealth of images of movement and adventure which it supplies.

With this difference in the material with which a child's fancy plays, there are other differences which turn on his temperament and predominant feelings. Hence, the familiar fact that in some children imagination broods by preference on gloomy and alarming objects, whereas in others it selects what is bright and gladsome.

Perhaps I have said enough to justify my plea for new observations and for a reconsideration of hasty theories in the light of these. Nor need we object to a fresh survey of what is perhaps the most delightful side of child-life.

(a) The Transforming Wand.

The play of young fancy meets us in the very domain of the senses : it is active, often bewilderingly active, when the small person seems busily engaged in looking at things and moving among them.

We see this fanciful "reading" of things when a

child calls the star an "eye," I suppose because of its brightness and its twinkling movement, or says that a dripping plant is "crying".

This transforming touch of the magic wand of young fancy has something of crude nature-poetry in it. This is abundantly illustrated in what may be called childish metaphors, by which they try to describe what is new and strange. For example, a little boy of nineteen months looking at his mother's spectacles said : "Little windows". Another boy two years and five months, on looking at the hammers of a piano which his mother was playing, called out : "There is owlegie" (diminutive of owl). His eye had instantly caught the similarity between the round felt disc of the hammer divided by a piece of wood, and the owl's face divided by its beak. In like manner another little boy called a small oscillating compass-needle a "bird" probably on the ground of its fluttering movement. Pretty conceits are often resorted to in this effort to get at home with strange objects, as when stars were described by one child as "cinders from God's stove," and butterflies as "pansies flying".

This play of imagination upon the world of sense has a strong vitalising or personifying element. A child is apt to attribute life and sensation to what we serious people regard as lifeless. Thus he gives not only a body but a soul to the wind when it whistles or howls at night. The most unpromising things come in for this warming, life-giving touch of a child's fancy. Thus one little fellow, aged one year eight months, conceived a special fondness for the letter W, address-ing it thus : "Dear old boy W". Miss Ingelow tells us that when a child she used to feel sorry for the pebbles in the causeway for having to lie always in one place, and would carry them to another place for a change.

It is hard for us elders to get back to this childish way of looking at things. One may however hazard the guess that there is in it a measure of dreamy illusion. This means that only a part of what is present is seen, the part which makes the new object like the old and familiar one. And so it gets transformed into a semblance of the old one; just as a rock gets transformed for our older eyes into the semblance of a human face.

There is another way in which children's fancy may transmute the objects of sense. Mr. Ruskin tells us that when young he got to connect or "associate" the name "crocodile" so closely with the creature that when he saw it printed it would take on something of the look of the beast's lanky body.

How far, one wonders, does this process of transformation of external objects go in the case of imaginative children? It is not improbable that before the qualities of things and their connections one with another are sufficiently known for them to be interesting in themselves they often acquire interest through the interpretative touch of childish fancy.

There is one new field of investigation which is illustrating in a curious way the wizard influence wielded by childish imagination over the things of sense. It is well known that a certain number of people habitually "colour" the sounds they hear, imagining, for example, the sound of a particular vowel or musical tone to have its characteristic tint, which they are able to describe accurately. This "coloured hearing," as it is called, is always traced back to the dimly recalled age of childhood. Children are now beginning to be tested as to their possession of this trick of fancy. It was found in the case of a number of school-children that nearly 40 per cent. described the tones of certain instruments as coloured. There was, however, no agreement among these children as to the particular tint belonging to a given sound : thus whereas one child mentally "saw" the tone of a fife as pale or bright, another saw it as dark.

I have confined myself here to what I have called the *play* of imagination, the magical transmuting of things through the sheer liveliness of childish fancy. The degree of transmutation will of course vary with the intensity of the imagination. Sometimes when a child dwells on the fancy it may grow into a momentary illusion. A little girl of four, sitting by the side of her mother in the garden, picked up a small pink worm and said : "Ah! you do look nice; how a thrush would like you!" and thereupon, realising the part of the fortunate thrush, proceeded, to her mother's horror, to eat up the worm quite composedly. The momentary illusion of something nice to eat, here produced by a lively realisation of a part, may arise in other cases from strong feeling, more especially fear, which, as we shall see, has so large a dominion over the young mind.

This witchcraft of the young fancy in veiling and transforming the actual surroundings is a good deal restrained by the practical needs of every-day life and by intercourse with older and graver folk. There are, however, regions of child-life where it knows no check. One of these is child's play, to be spoken of presently: another is the filling up of the blank spaces in the visible world with the products of fancy. We will call these regions on which the young wing of fancy is wont to alight and rest, fancy's resting-places.

Fancy's Resting-places.

Most people, perhaps, can recall from their childhood the pleasure of cloud-gazing. The clouds are such strange-looking things, they change their forms so quickly, they seem to be doing so many things, now slumbering lazily, now rushing wildly on. Cloud-land is safe away from the scrutiny of fingers, so we never can be sure what they would be if we got to them. Some children take fright at their big, strange forms and their weird transformations: but a happy child that loves day-dreaming will spend many delightful hours in fashioning these forms into wondrous and delightful things, such as kings and queens, giants and dwarfs, beautiful castles, armies marching to battle, or driven in flight, pirates sailing over fair isle-dotted seas. There is a delicious satisfaction to young minds in thus finding a habitation for their cherished images. To project them in this way into the visible world, to know that they are located in that spot before the eye, is to "realise" them, in the sense of giving them the fullest possible reality.

Next to the cloud-world come distant parts of the terrestrial scene. The chain of hills, perhaps, faintly visible from the home, has been again and again endowed by a child's fancy with all manner of wondrous scenery and peopled by all manner of strange creatures.

At times when they have shown a soft blue, he has made fairy-land of them ; at other times when standing out black and fierce-looking against the western sky at eventide, he has half shuddered at them, peopling them with horrid monsters.

Best of all, I think, for this locating of images, are the hidden spaces of the visible world. One child used to wonder what was hidden behind a long stretch of wood which closed in a good part of his horizon. Many a child has had his day-dreams about the country lying beyond the hills on the horizon. One little girl who lived on a cattle-station in Australia used to locate beyond a low range of hills a family of children whom she called her little girls, and about whom she related endless stories.

With timid children this tendency to project images into unseen places becomes a fearful kind of wonder, not altogether unpleasant when confined to a moderate intensity. I remember the look of awe on the face of a small boy whose hand I held as we passed one summer evening a dark wood, and he whispered to me that the wolves lived in that wood.

This impulse of timid children to project their dark fancies into obscure and hidden places often stops short at vague undefinable conjecture. "When (writes a German author) I was a child and we played hide and seek in the barn, I always felt that there must or might be something unheard of hidden away behind every bundle of straw, and in the corners." Here we can hardly speak of a housing of images : at such a moment perhaps the little brain has such a rush of weird images that no one grows distinct.

The exact opposite of this is where a child has a

very definite image in his mind, and wants to find a home for it in the external world. This wish seems to be particularly active in relation to the images derived from stories. This housing instinct is strong in the case of the poor houseless fairies. One little boy put his fairies in the wall of his bedroom, where, I suppose, he found it convenient to reach them by his prayers. His sister located a fairy in a hole in a smallish stone.

As with the fancies born of fairy-tales, so with the images of humbler human personages known by way of books. Charles Dickens, when a child, had a strong impulse to locate the characters of his stories in the immediate surroundings. He tells us that "every barn in the neighbourhood, every stone of the church, every foot of the churchyard had some association of its own in my mind connected with these books (*Roderic Random*, *Tom Jones*, *Gil Blas*, etc.), and stood for some locality made famous in them. I have seen Tom Pipes go climbing up the church steeple; I have watched Strap with the knapsack on his back stopping to rest himself on the wicket-gate."

In Storyland.

The reference to stories naturally brings us to another domain of children's imagination : the new world opened up by their story-books, which is all strange and far away from the nursery where they sit and listen, and in which, nevertheless, they manage in a sense to live and make a new home.

How is it, one is disposed to ask, that most children, at any rate, have their imagination laid hold of, and fired to a white heat, by mere words? To watch the small listener in its low chair, with head raised, eyes fixed, and hands clasped, drinking in every word of your story, giving sign by occasional self-cuddling and other spasmodic movements of the almost over-powering delight which fills its breast, is to be face to face with what is a mystery to most "grown-ups". Perhaps we elders, who are apt to think that we have acquired all the knowledge and to forget how much we have lost, will never understand the spell of a story for the lively impressionable brain of a child. One thing, however, is pretty certain : our words have a way of calling up in children's minds very vivid and very real images of things, images quite unlike those which are called up in the minds of most older people. This magic power of a word to summon the corresponding image, has, I suspect, a good deal to do with a child's intense way of realising his stories.

The passionate interest in stories means more than this however. It means that the little brain is wondrously deft at disentangling our rather hard language and reducing the underlying ideas to an intelligible simplicity. A mother when reading a poem to her boy of six, ventured to remark, " I'm afraid you can't understand it, dear," for which she got rather roughly snubbed by her little master in this fashion : "Oh, yes, I can very well, if only you would not explain ". The " explaining " is resented because it interrupts the child's own secret art of " making something " out of our words.

And what glorious inner visions the skilful little in-terpreter often manages to get from these troublesome words of ours. Scene after scene of the dissolving

2

view unfolds itself in definite outline and magical colouring. At each stage the anticipation of the next undiscernible stage is a thrilling mystery. Perhaps no one has given us a better account of the state of dream-like absorption in storyland than Thackeray. In one of his delightful " Roundabout Papers," he thus writes of the experiences of early boyhood : " Hush! I never read quite to the end of my first *Scottish Chiefs*. I couldn't. I peeped in an alarmed furtive manner at some of the closing pages. . . . Oh, novels, sweet and delicious as the raspberry open tarts of budding boyhood! Do I forget one night after prayers (when we under-boys were sent to bed) lingering at my cupboard to read one little half-page more of my dear Walter Scott—and down came the monitor's dictionary on my head !"

The intensity of the delight is seen in the greed it generates. Who can resist a child's hungry demand for a story ? and after you have satisfied his first request, he will ask for more, and if then you are weak enough to say you know no more stories he will catch you by answering : " Tell me the same again ".

As a result of the intensity with which a child's imagination seizes on a narrative it tends to become afterwards a record of fact, a true history. That children look at their stories in this way till they get undeceived seems to be shown by the respect which they pay to the details and even to the words. Woe to the unfortunate mother who in repeating one of the good stock nursery tales varies a detail. One such, a friend of mine, when relating " Puss in Boots " inadvertently made the hero sit on a chair instead of on a box to pull on his boots. She was greeted by a sharp volley of "Noes!"

As the demand for faithful repetition of story shows, the imaginative realisation continues when the story is no longer heard or read. It has added to the child's self-created world new territory, in which he may wander and live blissful moments. This permanent occupation of storyland is shown in the child's impulse to bring the figures of story-books into the actual surroundings. It is shown, too, in his fondness for introducing them into his play, of which I shall speak presently.

To this lively imaginative reception of what is told him the child is apt very soon to join his own free inventions of fairy and other tales. These at first, and for some time, have in them more of play than of serious art, and so can be touched on here where we are dealing with the play of young fancy.

We see the beginning of such fanciful invention in childish "romancing" which is often started by the sight of some real object. For example, a little boy aged three and a half years seeing a tramp limping along with a bad leg exclaimed : "Look at that poor ole man, mamma ; he has dot (got) a bad leg". Then romancing, as he was now wont to do : " He dot on a very big 'orse, and he fell off on some great big stone, and he hurt his poor leg and he had to get a big stick. We must make it well." Then after a thoughtful pause : "Mamma, go and kiss the place and put some powdey (powder) on it and make it well like you do to I ". Later on children of an imaginative turn wax bolder and spin longer stories and create scenes and persons with whom they live in

a prolonged companionship.   But of this more presently.

Partly by taking in and fully realising the wonders
of story, partly by a more spontaneous play of creative fancy, children's minds often pass under the
dominion of more or less enduring myths.   The princes
and princesses and dwarfs and gnomes of fairy-tale,
the generous but discriminating old gentleman who
brings Christmas presents, as well as the beings
fashioned by the more original sort of child for himself,
these live on just like the people of the every-day
world, are apt to appear in dreams, in the dark, at
odd dreamy moments during the day, bringing into
the child's life golden sunlight or black awful
shadows, and making in many cases, for a time at
least, the most real of all realities.

I am far from saying that *all* children make a fancy
world for themselves in this way.   As I said at the
beginning of the chapter the differences among children in this respect are great.   Yet I think it is safe
to say that most children, and especially lonely children who have not a full active life provided for
them by companions and opportunities of adventure,
do live a good fraction of their life in dreamland.

Where the active life is provided a child is apt to
play rather than lose himself passively in fancy
dreams.   But play, too, is to a large extent a product
of the liveliness of the young imagination.   We will
now glance at it in this light.

CHAPTER II.

THE ENCHANTMENT OF PLAY.

CHILDREN'S "play," as the expression is commonly understood, differs from the sportive movements of fancy considered in the last chapter by its essentially active character. We do not speak of a child playing save when he does something, however slight, by way of expressing or acting out a fancy. This outer expression of fancy in some active form is commonly called by children themselves "pretending" to be or to do something, by older people when looking back on the pretence "making-believe". In order to understand what childish fancy is like, and how it works, we must carefully watch it as it moves among the toys and creates a new play-world.

The Young Pretender.

Child's play is a kind of creation of a make-believe but half-real world. As such, it has its primal source in the impulse to act out and embody in sensible form some interesting idea; in which respect, as we shall see by-and-by, it has a close kinship to what we call art. The image, say of the wood, of the chivalrous highwayman, or what not, holds the child's brain, and everything has to accommodate itself to the mastering force.

Now since play is the acting out of some interesting and exciting fancy, it comes at once into collision with the child's actual surroundings. Here, however, he finds his opportunity. The floor of the room is magically transformed into a prairie, a sea, or other locality, the hidden space under the table becomes a robber's cave, a chair serves as horse, ship, or other vehicle, to suit the exigencies of the particular play.

The passion for play is essentially active; it is the wild longing to act a part; it is thus in a way dramatic. The child-adventurer as he personates Robinson Crusoe or other hero becomes another being. And in stepping, so to say, out of his every-day self he has to step out of his every-day world. Hence the transformation of his surroundings by what has been called the "alchemy of imagination". Even a sick child confined to his bed will, as Mr. Stevenson tells us in his pretty child's song, "The Land of Counterpane," make these transformations of his surroundings :—

And sometimes for an hour or so
I watched my leaden soldiers go,
With different uniforms and drills,
Among the bed-clothes through the hills;

And sometimes sent my ships in fleets,
All up and down among the sheets;
Or brought my trees and houses out,
And planted cities all about.

The impulse to act a part, which is the very life-breath of play, meets us in a crude form very early. Even an infant will, if there is a cup at hand, seem to go through something like a pretence of drinking. A little boy of about eighteen months who was digging in the garden began suddenly to play at having a bath. He got into the big bucket he was using for digging, took a handful of earth and dribbled it over him, saying, "'Ponge, 'ponge," and then stepped out and asked for " Tow'l, tow'l ". Another boy less than two would spend a whole wet afternoon enjoying his make-believe " painting " of the furniture with the dry end of a bit of rope.

There is no need to suppose that in this simple kind of imitative make-believe children *know* that they are acting a part. It is surely to misunderstand the essence of play to speak of it as a kind of conscious performance, like that of the stage-actor. A child is one creature when he is truly at play, another when he is bent on astonishing or amusing you. When absorbed in play the last thing he is thinking of is a spectator. As we know, the intrusion of a grown-up is very apt to mar children's play, by calling them back to the dull world of every-day.

This impulse to get away from his common and tiresome self into a new part will often carry a child rather far. Not only does he want to be a prince, or a fairy, he will even make an attempt to become an animal. He will greatly enjoy going on all fours and making dreadful noises if only he has a play-companion to be frightened ; and possibly he does get some way towards feeling like the bloodthirsty lion whom he fancies himself.

It is worth noting that such passing out of one's ordinary self and assuming a foreign existence is confined to the child-player. A cat or a dog will be quite ready to go through a kind of make-believe game, yet even in its play the cat remains the cat, and the dog the dog.

Such play-like transmutation of the self is sometimes carried over longer periods. A child will play at being something for a whole day. For example, a boy of three and a half years would one day lead the life of a coal-heaver, another day that of a soldier, and so forth, and was rather particular in expecting his mother to remember which of his favourite characters he was adopting on this or that day.

In a good deal of this play-action there is scarcely any adjustment of scene: the child of vigorous fancy plays out his part with imaginary surroundings. Children in their second year will act out a scene purely by means of pantomimic movements. Thus one little fellow not quite two years old would, when taken out in his perambulator, amuse himself by putting out his hand and pretending to catch "little micies" (mice), which make-believe little rodents he proceeded to cuddle and to stroke, winding up his play by throwing them away, or handing them over to his mother. In like manner he would pretend to feed chickens, taking imaginary food with one hand out of the other, and scattering it with an accompaniment of "Chuck! chuck! chuck!"

This tendency of the little player to conjure up new surroundings, and to bring to his side desirable companions, is, I suspect, common among lonely children. One little fellow of four passed much of his time in journeyings to Edinburgh, "London town," China and so forth in quest of his two little boys who roved about with their "mamsey," a "Mrs. Cock". They paid him visits when he was alone, always contriving to depart "just two tiny minutes" before any one came in.[1] Mr. Canton's little heroine took to nursing an invisible "iccle gaal" (little girl), of whose presence she seemed perfectly assured.[2]

If only the young imagination is strong enough there may be more of sweet illusion, of a warm grasp of living reality in this solitary play, where fictitious companions, perfectly obedient to the little player's will, take the place of less controllable ones. Yet this kind of play, which derives no support from the surroundings, makes heavy demands on the imagination, and would not, one suspects, satisfy most children.

The character of the little player's actual surroundings is, for the most part, a matter of small concern to him. If only he has a dark corner and a piece of furniture or two he can build his play-scene.

What he does want is some semblance of a living companion. Whatever his play he needs somebody, if only as listener to his make-believe ; and when his imagination cannot rise to an invisible auditor, he will talk to such unpromising things as a sponge in the bath, a fire-shovel, or a clothes-prop in the garden. In more active sorts of play, where something has to be done, he will commonly want a living companion.

In this making of play-companions we see again the transforming power of a child's fancy. Mr. Ruskin speaks somewhere of "the perfection of child-like imagination, the power of making everything out of nothing". This delightful secret of childhood is illustrated in its fondness for toys and its way of behaving towards them.

[1] From a paper by Mrs. Robert Jardine.
[2] *The Invisible Playmate*, p. 33 ff.

Later on, I think, children are apt to grow more sophisticated, to pay more attention to their surroundings, and to require more realistic accessories for their play actions.   This, at least Dr. Stanley Hall tells us, is true of doll-plays.

Mysteries of Dolldom.

The fact that children make living things out of their toy horses, dogs and the rest is known to every observer of their ways.   To the natural unsceptical eye the boy on his rudely carved " gee-gee" slashing the dull flank with all a boy's glee, looks as if he were possessed with the fancy that the rigid inert-looking block which he bestraddles is a very horse.

This breathing of life into playthings is seen in all its magic force in play with dolls.   A doll, broadly conceived, is anything which a child carries about and makes a pet of.   The toy horse, dog or what not that a little boy nurses, feeds and takes to bed with him has much of the dignity of a true doll.   But adopting conventional distinctions we shall confine the word to those things which are more or less endowed by childish fancy with human form and character.

I read somewhere recently that the doll is a plaything for girls only: but young boys, though they often prefer india-rubber horses and other animals, not infrequently go through a stage of doll-love also, and are hardly less devoted than girls.

Endless is the variety of *rôle* assigned to the doll. It is the all-important comrade in that *solitude à deux* of which the child, like the adult, is so fond.   Mrs.

Burnett tells us that when nursing her doll in the armchair of the parlour she would sail across enchanted seas to enchanted islands having all sorts of thrilling adventures.

Very tenderly, on the whole, is the little doll-lover wont to use her pet, doing her best to keep it clean and tidy, feeding it, putting it to bed, amusing it, for example, by showing it her pictures, tending it with fidelity during bouts of sickness, and giving it the honours of a funeral when, from the attack of a dog set on by an unfeeling brother or other cause, it comes to " die " ;[1] or when, as in the case of little Jane Welsh (afterwards Mrs. Carlyle), the time has come for the young lady to cast aside her dolls.

The doll-interest implies a deep mysterious sympathy. Children wish their dolls to share in their things, to be kissed when they are kissed, and so to come close to them in experience and feeling. Not only so, they look for sympathy from their doll-companions, taking to them all their childish troubles. So far is this feeling of oneness carried in some cases that the passion for dolls has actually rendered the child indifferent to child-companions. It is not every little girl who like little Maggie Tulliver has only "occasional fits of fondness" for her nursling when the brother is absent.

Not only in this lavishing of tenderness and of sympathy on the doll, but in the occasional discharge on it of a fit of anger, children show how near it comes to a human companion. The punishment of the doll

---

[1] I owe this and other observations on the treatment of dolls to Dr. Stanley Hall's curious researches.

is an important element in nursery-life. It is apt to be carried out with formal solemnity and often with something of brutal emphasis. Yet tenderness being the strongest part of the doll-attachment, the little disciplinarians are apt to suffer afterwards for their cruelty, one little girl showing remorse after such a chastisement of her pet for several days.

I have talked here of "dolls," but I must not be supposed to be speaking merely of the lovely creatures with blue eyes and yellow hair with which the well-to-do child is wont to be supplied. Nothing is more strange and curious in child-life than its art of manufacturing dolls out of the most unpromising materials. The creative child can find something to nurse and fondle and take to bed with it in a bundle of hay tied round with a string, in a shawl, a pillow, a stick, a clothes-pin, or a clay-pipe. Victor Hugo, with a true touch, makes the little outcast Cosette, who has never had a "real doll," fashion one out of a tiny leaden sword and a rag or two, putting it to sleep in her arms with a soft lullaby.

Do any of us really understand the child's attitude of mind towards its doll? Although gifted writers like George Sand have tried to take us back to the feeling of childhood, it may be doubted whether they have made it intelligible to us. And certainly the answers to questions collected in America have done little, if anything, towards making it clear. The truth is that the perfect child's faith in dolldom passes away early, in most cases it would appear about the age of thirteen or fourteen. It is then that the young people begin clearly to realise the shocking fact that dolls have no "inner life". Occasionally girls will go on playing with dolls much later than this, but not surely with the old sincerity.

That many children have a genuine delusion about their dolls seems evident. That is to say when they talk to them and otherwise treat them as human they imaginatively realise that they can understand and feel. The force of the illusion, blotting out from the child's view the naked reality before its eyes, is a striking illustration of the vividness of early fancy. Perhaps, too, this intensity of faith comes in part of the strength of the impulses which commonly sustain the doll-passion. Of these the instinct of companionship, of sympathy, is the strongest. A lady tells me she remembers that when a child she had a passionate longing for a big, big doll, which would give her the full sweetness of cuddling. The imitative impulse, too, prompting the child to carry out on the doll actions similar to those carried out on itself by mother and nurse, is a strong support of the delusion. A doll, as the odd varieties selected show, seems to be, more than anything else, something to be dressed. Children's reasons for preferring one doll to another, as that it can have its face washed, or that it has real hair which can be combed, show how the impulse to carry out nursery operations sustains the feeling of attachment. A girl (the same that wanted the big doll to fondle) had dolls of the proper sort ; yet she preferred to make one out of a little wooden stool, because she could more realistically act out with this odd substitute the experience of taking her pet out for a walk, making it stand, for example, when she met a friend.

Of course, the child's faith, like other faith, is not

always up to the height of perfect ardour. A child of six or seven, when the passion for dolls is apt to be strong, will have moments of coolness, leaving "poor dolly" lying in the most humiliating posture on the floor, or throwing it away in a sudden fit of disenchantment and disgust. Scepticism will intrude, especially when the hidden "inside" comes to view as mere emptiness, or at best as nothing but sawdust.

Children seem, as George Sand says, to oscillate between the real and the impossible. Yet the intrusion of doubt does not, in many cases at least, interfere with an enduring trust. Dr. Stanley Hall tells us that "long after it is *known* that they are wood, wax, etc., it is *felt* that they are of skin, flesh, etc.". Yes, that is it; the child, seized with the genuine play-mood, *dreams* its doll into a living child, or living adult. How oddly the player's faith goes on living side by side with a measure of doubt is illustrated in the following story. A little girl begged her mother not to make remarks about her doll in her (the doll's) presence, as she had been trying all her life to keep that doll from knowing that she was not alive.[1]

The treating of the doll and images of animals, such as the wooden or india-rubber horse, as living things is the outcome of the play-impulse. All the imaginative play of children seems, so far as we can understand it, to have about it something of illusion. This fact of the full sincere acceptance of the play-world as for the moment the real one, is illustrated in the child's jealous insistence that everything shall for the time pass over from the every-day world into the new one. "About

[1] From an article on "The Philosophy of Dolls," *Chambers' Journal*, 1881.

the age of four," writes M. Egger of his boys, " Felix is playing at being coachman ; Emile happens to return home at the moment. In announcing his brother, Felix does not say, 'Emile is come ;' he says, 'The brother of the coachman is come'." It is illustrated further in the keen resentment of any act on the part of the mother or other person which seems to contradict the facts of the new world. A boy of two who was playing one morning in his mother's bed at drinking up pussy's milk from an imaginary saucer on the pillow, said a little crossly to his mother, who was getting into bed after fetching his toys : " Don't lie on de saucer, mammy ! " The pain inflicted on the little player by such a contradictory action is sometimes intense. A little girl of four was playing " shops " with her younger sister. " The elder one (writes the mother) was shopman at the time I came into her room and kissed her. She broke out into piteous sobs, I could not understand why. At last she sobbed out : 'Mother, you never kiss the man in the shop'. I had with my kiss quite spoilt her illusion."

But there is still another, and some will think a more conclusive way of satisfying ourselves of the reality of the play-illusion. The child finds himself confronted by the unbeliever who questions what he says about the doll's crying and so forth, and in this case he will often stoutly defend his creed. " Discussions with sceptical brothers (writes Dr. Stanley Hall), who assert that the doll is nothing but wood, rubber, wax, etc., are often met with a resentment as keen as that vented upon missionaries who declare that idols are but stocks and stones." It is the same with the toy-horse. " When (writes a mother of her

boy) he was just over two years old L. began to speak
of a favourite wooden horse (Dobbin) as if it were a
real living creature. 'No tarpenter (carpenter) made
Dobbin,' he would say, 'he is not wooden but kin
(skin) and bones and Dod (God) made him.' If any
one said 'it' in speaking of the horse his wrath was
instantly aroused, and he would shout indignantly:
'It! You mut'ent tay *it*, you mut tay *he*.'"

While play in its absorbing moments, and even
afterwards, may thus produce a genuine illusion, the
state of perfect realisation is of course apt to be broken
by intervals of scepticism. This has already been
illustrated in the case of the doll. The same little
boy that played with the imaginary mice was sitting
on his stool pretending to smoke like his grandpapa
out of a bit of bent cardboard. Suddenly his face
clouded over ; he stroked his chin, and remarked in
a disappointed tone, " I have not got any whiskers ".
The dream of full manhood was here rudely dispelled
by a recall to reality.

A measure of the same fanciful transformation of
things that has been illustrated in make-believe play,
a measure, too, of the illusion which frequently ac-
companies it, enters, I believe, into all children's pas-
times. Whence comes the perennial charm, the un-
dying popularity, of the hoop? Is not the interest
here due to the circumstance that the child controls a
thing which in the freedom of its movements suggests
that it has a will of its own? This seems borne out
by the following story. A little girl of five once
stopped trundling her hoop and said to her mother she
thought that her hoop must be alive, because " it is so
sensible; it goes where I want it to ". Perhaps the

same thing may be said of other toys, as the kite and the sailing boat.   .

Serious Side of Play.

I have here treated the whole realm of childish fancy as one of play, as one in which happy childhood finds its own sunny world.   Yet it is clear that this is after all only one side of children's dreamworld.   Like our own world it has its climates, and if fancy is often frolicsome and games deliciously sweet, they sometimes become serious to the point of a quite dreadful solemnity.

That children's imagination is wont to hover, with something of the fascination of the moth, on the confines of the fearful, is known to us all.   Some children, no doubt, have much more of the passion for the gruesome and blood-curdling than others, since temperament counts for much here ; yet it is pretty safe to say that most know something of this horrible fascination.   Dreams, whether of the night or of the day, are not always of beautiful fairies and the like. Weird, awful-looking figures have a way of pushing themselves into the front of the scene.   Especially when the "tone" of the frail young nerves runs down from poor health do these alarming shapes appear, and acquire a mighty hold on the child's imagination.   Of the timidity of the early years of life I shall have more to say by-and-by.   Here I want to bring out how the very vividness of children's images exposes them to what is sometimes at least their worst form of suffering.

A child, at once sensitive and imaginative, frequently passes into a state of half hallucination in

3

which the products of fancy take on visible reality. George Sand, in her delightful reminiscences of childhood, relates more than one of these terrible prostrating hallucinations of the early years.[1]

We see the same gloomy turn of the young imagination in the readiness with which children accept superstitions about ghosts, witches, and so forth. Those who are brought up in the country in contact with the superstitious beliefs of the peasant appear to imbibe them with great energy. This is true of George Sand, who gives us an interesting account of the legends of the French peasants, with whom when a little girl she was allowed to associate. American children, especially those who come under the influence of the beliefs of the negro and of the Indian, may, as that delightful book, *Tom Sawyer*, tells us, become quite experts in folk-lore. Even in England and among well-to-do people children will show an alarming facility in adopting the superstitious ideas of the servants.

Much the same thing shows itself in children's romancings and in their preferences in the matter of stories. So far from these being always bright and amusing, they frequently show a very decided tinge of blackness. The young imagination seems to be especially plastic under the touch of the gruesome. It loves to be roused to its highest pitch of activity by the presentation of something fearsome, something which sends a wild tremor through the nerves. And even when the story is free from this touch of the dreadful it takes

[1] See my account of George Sand's childhood, in *Studies of Childhood*, chap. xii.

on seriousness by reason of the earnestness which the child's mind brings to it.

Coming now to active play, we find here, too, in the region which seems to owe its very existence to the childish instinct of enjoyment, traces of the same seriousness. For most children, one suspects, play would become a tame thing were there not the fearful to conjure with. The favourite play-haunts, the dark corners under the table, behind the curtains, and so forth, show what a vital element of play is supplied by the excitement of the state of half-dread. It is in the games which set the young nerves gently shaking, when a robber has to be met or a giant attacked in his cave, that one sees best, I think, how terribly earnest children's play may become.

Even where play has in it nothing alarming it is apt to take on a serious aspect. This has been illustrated in what has been said about the doll and other play-illusions. Most of children's play is imitative of the serious actions of grown-up folk. In nursing her doll the little girl is taking to her domestic duties in the most serious of moods; similarly when the little boy assumes the responsibilities of coachman or other useful functionary. The imitative impulse of childhood is wont in these cases to follow out the correct and prescribed order with punctilious exactness. The doll must be dressed, fed, put to bed, and so forth, with the regularity that obtains in the child's own life ; the coachman must hold the whip, urge on the horses, or stop them in the proper orthodox manner. And the same fidelity to model and prescription shows itself in those games which reproduce the page of

fiction.   Here again Tom Sawyer is an excellent
example.   The way in which that leader of boys lays
down the law to Huckleberry Finn when they play
at pirates or at Robin Hood and his merry men
illustrates forcibly this serious aspect of play.

PART II.

AT WORK.

CHAPTER III.

ATTACKING OUR LANGUAGE.

No part of the life of a child appeals to us more powerfully perhaps than the first use of our language. The small person's first efforts in linguistics win us by a certain graciousness, by the friendly impulse they disclose to get mentally near us, to enter into the full fruition of human intercourse. The difficulties, too, which we manage to lay upon the young learner of our tongue, and the way in which he grapples with these, lend a peculiar interest, half pathetic, half humorous, to this field of infantile activity. A child first begins to work in downright earnest when he tries to master these difficulties.

As we are here studying the child at an age when he has acquired a certain hold on human speech, I shall make no attempt to describe the babbling of the first months which precedes true speech. For the same reason I shall have to pass by the interesting beginnings of sign-making, and shall only just touch the first stages of articulate performance. All this is, I think, deeply interesting, but it cannot be adequately dealt with here, and I have fully dealt with it in my larger work.

The first difficulty which our little linguist has to encounter is the mechanical one of reproducing, with a recognisable measure of approximation, our verbal sounds. What a very rough approximation it is at first, all mothers know. When, for example, a child expects you to translate his sound "koppa" into "Tommy," or "pots" into "hippopotamus," it will be acknowledged that he is making heavy demands. Yet though he causes us difficulties in this way he does so because he finds himself in difficulties. His articulatory organ cannot master the terrible words we put in his way, and he is driven to these short cuts and other make-shifts.

The Namer of Things.

Leaving now the problem of getting over the mechanical difficulties of our speech, let us see what the little explorer has to do when trying to use verbal sounds with their right meanings. Here, too, we shall find that huge difficulties beset his path, and that his arrival at the goal proves him to have been in his way as valiant and hard-working as an African explorer.

One feature of the early tussle with our language is curious and often quaintly pretty. Having at first but few names, the little experimenter makes the most of these by extending them in new and surprising directions. The extension of names to new objects on the ground of some perceived likeness has been touched on above (p. 3); and many other examples might be given. Thus when one child first saw a star and wanted to name it he called it, as if by a poetic metaphor, an "eye". In like manner the name "pin" was extended by another child to a crumb just picked up, a fly, and a caterpillar, and seemed to mean something little to be taken between the fingers. The same child used the sound "'at" (hat) for anything put on the head, including a hair-brush. Similarly children often extend the names "Mamma, baby" to express any contrast of size, as when a small coin was called by an American child a "baby dollar".

In this extension of language by the child we find not merely a tendency to move along lines of analogy, as in the above instances, but to go from a thing to its accompaniments by way of what the psychologist calls association. This is illustrated by the case of Darwin's grandchild, who after learning to use the common children's name for duck, "quack," proceeded to call a sheet of water "quack". In like manner a little girl called the gas lamp "pop" from the sound produced when lighting it, and then carried over the name "pop" to the stool on which the maid stood when proceeding to light it.

There is another curious way in which children are driven by the slenderness of their verbal resources to "extend" the names they learn. They will often employ a word which indicates some relation to express what may be called the inverted relation. For example, like the unschooled yokel they will sometimes make the word "learn" do duty for "teach" also. In one case "spend" was made to express "cost". It was a somewhat similar inversion when a little girl called her parasol blown about by the wind "a windy parasol," and a stone that made her hand sore "a very sore stone".

Not only do the small experimenters thus stretch the application of their words beyond our conventional limitations, they are often daring enough when their stock fails them to invent new names. Sometimes this is done by framing a new composite name out of familiar ones. One child, for example, possessing the word steam-ship and wanting the name sailing-ship, cleverly hit upon the composite form "wind-ship". One little girl, when only a year and nine months old, showed quite a passion for classing objects by help of such compound names, arranging the rooms, for example, into "morner-room," "dinner-room" (she was fond of adding "er" at this time) and "nursery-room". Savages do much the same kind of thing, as when the Aztecs called a boat a "water-house".

It is no less bold a feat when the hard-pressed tyro in speechland frames a new word on the model of other words which he already knows. The results are often quaint enough. One small boy talked of the "rainer," the fairy who makes rain, and another little boy dubbed a teacher the "lessoner". Two children invented the quaint substantive "thinks" for "thoughts," and another child used the form "digs" for holes dug in the ground. Other droll inventions occur, as when one small person asked to see another worm "deading," and neatly expressed the act of undoing a parcel by the form "unparcel"; and when another child spoke of his metal toy being "unhotted," lacking our word cooled, and asked, "Can't I be sorried?" for "Can't I be forgiven?"

Just as children invent new general names, so they now and again invent "proper" names in order to mark off one person or thing from another of the same kind. Thus a German professor tells us that his grand-niece introduced her new nurse, who had the same name, "Mary," as her old one, as "Evening Mary," because she had arrived in the evening.

Of course children's experiments in language are not always so neat as this. They are sometimes misled by false analogies into the formation of such clumsy words as "sorrified" for "sorry," and "magnicious" for "magnificent".

The Sentence-builder.

It is an interesting moment when the young linguist tries his hand at putting words together in sentences. As is pretty well known, a child has for some time to try to make known his thoughts and wishes by single vocables, such as "mamma," "milk," "puss," "up," and so forth. Each of these words serves in the first baby language for a variety of sentences. Thus "Puss!" means sometimes "Puss is doing something," at other times "I want puss," and so forth. But somewhere about the age of one year nine months the child makes bold to essay a more explicit and definite form of statement.

The construction of sentences proceeds in a cautious manner. At first the structure is of the simplest, two words being placed one after the other, in what is called apposition, as in the couple, "Big bir" (big bird), "Papa no" (papa's nose), and the like.

Later on longer sentences are attempted of a similar

pattern ; and it is truly wonderful how much the child manages to express in this rude fashion without any aid from those valuable auxiliaries, prepositions, and the like. For example, one boy when in his twentieth month gave this elaborate order to his father, " Dada toe toe ba," that is, " Dada is to go and put his toes in the bath ".

Quaint inversions of our order not infrequently occur in this early sentence-making. Thus one child used the form, " Out-pull-baby 'pecs," meaning in our language, "Baby pulls (or will pull) out the spectacles". Sometimes the order reminds us still more closely of the idiom of foreign languages, as when a little girl said: " How Babba (baby, *i.e.*, herself) does feed nicely !"

Another curious feature of children's first style of composition is the fondness for antithesis. A little boy used when wishing to express his approval of something, say a dog, to use the form, " This a nice bow-wow, not nasty bow-bow ". Similarly a little girl said, " Boo (the name of her cat) dot (got) tail ; poor Babba (baby) dot no tail," proceeding to search for a tail under her skirts.

In the first attempts to fit our words together dreadful slips are apt to occur. The way in which children are wont to violate the rules of grammar when using verbs, as in saying "eated" for "ate," "scram " for "screamed,' " be'd " for "was," and so on, is well known, and there are many excuses to be found for these very natural errors.

Particularly instructive are the odd confusions which children are apt to fall into when they come to use the pronouns, and more particularly " I," "me". Many a child begins by using "I" and "you" with mechanical imitation of others, meaning by "you" his own person, which is, of course, called "you" by others when addressing him. The forms "I," "me" and "my" are apt to be hopelessly mixed up, as in saying "me go" and "my go" for "I go," "me book" for "my book," and so forth. One little boy used the form "I am" for "I," saying, for example, "I am don't want to". A little German girl had an odd way of splitting up herself into two persons, saying, for example, "She has made me wet," meaning that she had made herself wet.

Throughout this work of mastering our language a child is wont to eke out his deficiencies by bold strokes of originality. When, for example, a little girl towards the end of the second year, after being jumped by her father, wants him to jump her mother also, says, in default of the word "jump," "Make mamma high". Robert Hamerling, the Austrian poet, when a child, being told by his sick mother that he had not said something she wished him to say, answered, "I said it, but you didn't hear, you are poorly, and so *blind in the ear*". Quite pretty metaphors are sometimes hit upon, as when a little boy of two seeing his father putting a piece of wood on the fire said, "Flame going to eat it". A boy of twenty-seven months ingeniously said, "It rains off," for "The rain has left off". Once a girl about the same age as the boy hit on the idiom, "No two 'tatoes left," for "Only one potato is left". Pretty constructions sometimes appear in these make-shifts, as when a little girl of whom Mrs. Meynell tells, wishing to know how far she might go in spending money on fruit, asked, "What mustn't it be more than?"

The Interpreter of Words.

. There is one part of this task of mastering our language which deserves especial notice, *viz.*, the puzzling out of the meanings we put, or try to put, into our words.

Many good stories of children show that they have a way of sadly misunderstanding our words. This arises often from the ignorance of the child and the narrowness of his experience, as when a Sunday school scholar understood the story of the good Samaritan to mean that a gentleman came and poured some paraffin (*i.e.*, oil) over the poor man. By a child's mind what we call accidentals often get taken to be the real meaning. A boy and a girl, twins, had been dressed alike. Later on the boy was put into a "suit". A lady asked the girl about this time whether they were not the twins, when she replied, "No, we *used* to be". "Twin" was inseparably associated in her mind with the similarity in dress.

It should be remembered, too, that we greatly add to the difficulties of the small student of our language by reason of the ambiguities of our expressions, and of our short and elliptical modes of speaking. It was a quite natural misconception when an American child, noting that children were "half price" at a certain show, wanted his mother to get a baby now that they were cheap. Many another child besides Jean Ingelow has been saddened at being told by her father or other grown-up who was dancing her on his knee that he must put her down as he "had a bone in his leg". Much misapprehension arises, too from our figurative use of language, which the little listener is apt to interpret in a very literal way, as when a small boy indignantly resented the statement of his mother who was driving him behind a rather skittish pony, " Pony has lost his head ".

Children are desirous of understanding us and make brave efforts to put meanings into our words, sometimes falling comically short of the mark. A little fellow of two who had been called " fat " by his nurse when given his bath, afterwards proceeded to call his father " fat " when he saw him taking his bath. " Fat " had by a natural misconception taken on the meaning of " naked ". It was a simple movement of childish thought when a little school-girl answered the question of the Inspector, " What is an average ? " by saying, " What the hen lays eggs on ". She had heard her mother say, " The hen lays so many eggs ' on the average ' every week," and had no doubt imagined a little myth about this average.

It is the same with what is read to them. Where they do not recognise a meaning they invent one, or if necessary substitute an intelligible word for an unintelligible one. Young Hermiston in R. L. Stevenson's last story naturally enough said in speaking of his father, the " hanging judge," " It were better for that man if a *milestone* were bound about his neck". Similarly they will invert the relations of words in order to arrive at something like a meaning. Mr. Canton relates in his pretty sketch of a child, *The Invisible Playmate*, that his little heroine, who knew the lines in *Struwwelpeter*—

> The doctor came and shook his head,
> And gave him nasty physic too—

was told that she would catch a cold, and that she at once replied, " And will the doctor come and shook my head? " It was so much more natural to suppose that when the doctor came and did something this was carried out on the person of the patient.

There is something of this same impatience of meaningless sayings, of the same keen desire to import a meaning into strange words, in children's " word-play," as we call it. For example, a little boy about four years old heard his mother speak of nurse's neuralgia, from which she had been suffering for some time. He thereupon exclaimed, " I don't think it's *new* ralgia, I call it *old* ralgia ". Was this playful punning or a half-serious attempt to correct a misstatement? A child called his doll " Shakespeare " because its spear-like legs could be shaken. We know that adults sometimes do the same kind of thing, as a cabman I once overheard speaking to somebody about putting down " *ash*phalt ". We all like to feel at home with words, and if they look dreadfully strange we do our best to give them a look of old acquaintance.

It should be added that children, though they eke out their deficiencies by inventing new verbal forms and putting new meanings into our words, have on the whole a vast respect for words. This is seen in their way of stickling for accuracy when others repeat familiar word-forms. The zeal of a child in correcting the language not only of other children, but of grown-ups, and the comical errors he will now and again fall into in exercising his corrective function, are well known to parents. Sometimes he shows himself the most absurd of pedants. " Shall I read to you out of this book, baby?" asked a mother of her boy, about two and a half years old. "No," replied the infant, "not *out* of dot book, but somepy inside of it." The same little stickler for verbal accuracy, when his nurse asked him, "Are you going to build your bricks, baby?" replied solemnly, "We don't build bricks, we make them and then build *with* them". Yet such disagreeable pedantry shows how conscientiously the small curly head is trying to bring clearness and order into the dark tangle of our speech, and it ought not to be treated harshly.

CHAPTER IV.

THE SERIOUS SEARCHER.

In a former chapter we dealt with a child's mind as a harbourer of fancies, as subject to the illusive spell of its bright imagery. Yet with this play of fancy there goes a respectable quantity of serious inquiry into the things of the real world. This is true, I believe, even of highly imaginative children, who now and again come down from their fancy-created world and regard the solid matter-of-fact one at their feet with shrewdly scrutinising eyes. For children, like some of those patients of whom the hypnotist tells us, live alternately two lives.

The child not only scans his surroundings, he begins to reflect on what he observes, and does his best to understand the puzzling scene which meets his eyes. And all this gives seriousness, a deep and admirable seriousness, to his attitude; so that one may forgive the touch of exaggeration when Mr. Bret Harte writes: "All those who have made a loving study of the young human animal will, I think, admit that its dominant expression is *gravity* and not playfulness". We may now turn to this graver side of the young intelligence.

The Thoughtful Observer.

This serious examination of things begins early.

Most of us have been subjected to the searching gaze of an infant's eyes when we first made it overtures of friendship. How much this fixed gaze of a child of six months takes in nobody can say.

What we find when the child grows and can give an account of his observations is that, while often surprisingly minute in particular directions, they are narrowly confined. Thus a child will sometimes be so impressed with the colour of an object as almost to ignore its form. A little girl of eighteen months, who knew lambs and called them "lammies," on seeing two black ones in a field among some white ones called out, " Eh! doggie, doggie! " The likeness of colour to the black dog overpowered the likeness in form to the other lambs close by. We shall find further examples of this one-sided observation when we come to consider children's drawings.

The pressure of practical needs tends, however, to develop a fuller examination of objects. A lamb and a dog, for example, have to be distinguished by a number of marks in which the supremely interesting detail of colour holds a quite subordinate place. Individual things, too, have to be more carefully distinguished, if only for the purpose of drawing the line between what is " mine " and " not mine," for example, spoons and picture-books. The recognition of the mother, say, exacts this fuller inspection, for she cannot always be recognised by her height alone, for example, when she is sitting, nor by her hair alone, as when she has her hat on, so that *a group* of distinctive features has to be seized.

When once the eye has begun to note differences it makes rapid progress. This is particularly true

4

where the development of a special interest leads to a habit of concentration on a particular kind of object. Thus little boys when the "railway interest" seizes them are apt to be finely observant of the differences between this and that engine and so forth. A boy aged two years and eleven months, after travelling over two railways, asked his mother if she had noticed the difference in the make of the rails on the two lines. Of course she had not, though she afterwards ascertained that there was a slight difference which the boy's keener eyes had detected.

The fineness of children's distinguishing observation is well illustrated in their recognition of small drawings and photographs, as when one child of two instantly picked out the likeness of his father from a small *carte de visite* group.

In truth, children's observation, when close and prolonged, as it is apt to be under the stimulus of a really powerful interest, is often surprisingly full as well as exact. The boy, John Ruskin, could look for hours together at flowing water, noting all its subtle changes. Another little boy, when three and a half years old, received a picture-book, *The Railway Train*, and inspected the drawings almost uninterruptedly for a week, retaining the treasure even at meals. "At the end of this time (writes his mother) he had grasped the smallest detail in every picture."

Along with this serious work of observing things there often goes a particularly bright and exact recollection of them and their names. Feats of memory in the first three years are, I suspect, a common theme of discourse among admiring mothers. Here is a sample of many stories sent me. A little girl only nine months old when taken out for a walk was shown some lambs at the gate of a field. On being taken the same road three weeks later she surprised her mother by calling out just before arriving at the gate, "Baa, baa!" Later on children will remember through much longer intervals. A little boy of two years on seeing a girl cousin who lived in the country where he had visited five months before, at once asked whether her dog "Bruce" barked. Another boy aged two years and ten months on revisiting his mother's paternal home in Italy after four or five months remembered small details, *e.g.*, how the grapes were cut, and how the wine was made.

Nor does the busy brain of the child stop at observing and recalling what lies about him. He begins at an early age to compare this thing with that, and to note the relations and connections of things, how he is almost as tall as the table, for example, and a good deal taller than pussy, how he has a spoon while his elders have knives and forks, and so forth. And all the while he is trying to get at the general rule or law which obtains in this and that realm of things.

The first attempts of a child to grasp the causal connections of things are apt to be quaint enough. Professor Preyer tells us that his little boy, having been told to blow on his hand which had been hurt, proceeded afterwards when he had struck his head against something "to blow of his own accord, supposing that the blowing would have a soothing effect, even when it did not reach the injured part".[1]

---

[1] *The Development of the Intellect* (Appleton & Co.), p. 155.

Since the little searcher in trying to piece his facts together in their proper connections must, as all of us do, make use of such experiences as he happens to have, he will pretty certainly fall into the error of " hasty generalisation," as we call it, taking things to be really connected which accidentally occur together, it may be in a single instance only. An American boy of ten who had happened to have a teacher who was short and cross, and a second who was tall and very kind, said to his new teacher, who struck him as short, "I'm afraid you'll make a cross teacher". Yet while we smile at such simplicity ought we not to remember that older people, too, sometimes commit similar blunders, and that after all the impulse to reason can only work itself into a good sound faculty by risking such blunders ?

The Pertinacious Questioner.

The effort of the child to understand the things about him grows noteworthy somewhere near the end of the third year, and about the same time there comes the questioning " mania," as we are apt to regard it. The first question was put in the case of a boy in the twenty-eighth month, in the case of a girl in the twenty-third month. But the true age of inquisitiveness when questions are fired off with wondrous rapidity and pertinacity seems to be ushered in with the fourth year.

A common theory peculiarly favoured by ignorant nurses and mothers is that children's questioning is one of the ways in which they love to plague their elders. We shall see presently how much truth there

is in this view.   It may be enough here to say that a
good deal of this first questioning is something very
different.   A child asks you what this thing is you
wear on your watch-chain, why you part your hair in
the middle, or what not, because he feels that he is
ignorant, and for the moment at any rate he would
like to get his ignorance removed.   More than this,
his question shows that he thinks you can satisfy his
curiosity.

Questioning may take various directions.   A good
deal of the child's catechising of his long-suffering
mother is prompted by a more or less keen desire for
fact.   The typical form of this line of questioning is
"What?"   The motive here is commonly the wish to
know something which will connect itself with and
complete a bit of knowledge already gained.   "How
old is Rover?"   "Where was Rover born?"   "Who
was his father?"   "What is that dog's name?"
"What sort of hair had you when you were a little
girl?"   This kind of questioning may spring out of
pure childish curiosity, or out of some practical need,
as that of acting out a part in play.   Thus a Kindergarten teacher was wont to be besieged with questions
of this kind from her small boys when playing at
being animals: "Do walruses swim fast or slow?"
"Do lions climb trees?"

One feature in this pursuit of fact is the great store
which a child sets by names of things.   It has been
pointed out by a French writer that the form of question: "What is this?" often means, "What is it
called?"   A child is apt to think that everything has
its own name.   One little boy explained to his mother
that he thought all the frogs, the mice, the birds and

the butterflies had names given to them by their
mothers, just as babies have.   Perhaps children when
they find out the name of a new thing feel that they
know it, that they have been introduced to it, so to
speak.

Another motive in this early questioning is the
desire for an explanation of what is seen or heard
about the reason and the cause of things.   It takes
the well-known forms, "Why?" "Who made?" and
so forth.   Who that has tried to instruct the small
child of three or four does not know the long shrill
whine-like sound of this question?

Nothing perhaps in child utterance is better worth
interpreting, hardly anything more difficult to interpret, than this simple-looking little "why?"

Let us in judging of this pitiless "why?" try to
understand the situation of the small searcher confronted by so much that is strange and puzzling in
nature, and in human life alike.   Just because he is
born a thinker he must try at least to bring the
strange thing into some connection with his familiar
world.   And what is more natural than to go to the
wise lips of the grown-up for a solution of the
difficulty?

The demand for the reason or explanation of a
thing may be satisfied by a bare reference to some
other thing which is similar and so fitted to throw the
light of familiarity on what is new and strange.   For
example, you may sometimes still a child's questioning as to why pussy has fur by telling him that it is
pussy's hair.   A child may find an appeasement, too,
of his logical appetite in learning that what is new
and strange to him comes under a general rule, that,

for example, many other animals besides pussy have fur.

Nevertheless, I suspect that a child's "why?" aims farther than this; that it is only fully appeased by a knowledge of what we older folk call a reason, that is to say of the cause which originates a thing, and of the purpose which it serves. It is easy to see, indeed, that this questioning curiosity of the little ones is largely directed to the subject of origins or makings. What hours and hours do they not spend in wondering how the pebbles, the stones, the birds, the babies are made!

The inquiry into origin starts with the amiable presupposition that all things have been produced by hand-craft after the manner of household possessions. The world is a sort of big house where everything has been made by somebody, or at least fetched from somewhere. And this is perhaps natural enough, for of the things whose production the child sees are not the larger number fashioned by human hands? He him-self makes a considerable number of things, including these rents in his clothes, messes on the tablecloth, and the like, which he gets firmly imprinted on his memory by the authorities. And, then, he is wont to watch with a keen interest the making of things by others, such as puddings, clothes, houses, hay-ricks. To ask, then, who made the animals, the babies, the wind, the clouds, and so forth, is for him merely to apply the type of causation which is familiar to him.

The demand for a reason takes on a more special meaning when the idea of purpose becomes clear. The search now is for the use of a thing, the end which the maker had in view when he fashioned it

When, for example, a child asks, " Why is there such a lot of dust?" he seems to be seeking the purpose which the maker of dust had in mind, or in other words the use of dust. Similarly when things are endowed with life and their own purpose, as in asking, " Why does the wind blow?" Here the child thinks of nature's processes as if they were a kind of human action which we can understand by seeing into its aim.

Here are some curious observations which seem to illustrate this childish idea of how nature's processes originate. A little girl whom we will call M., when one year eleven months old, happened to be walking with her mother on a windy day. At first she was delighted at the strong boisterous wind, but then got tired and said: " Wind make mamma's hair untidy, Babba (her own name) make mamma's hair tidy, *so wind not blow adain* (again) ". About three weeks later the same child being out in the rain with her mother said : " Mamma, dy (dry) Babba's hands, *so not rain any more*". This little inquirer seems clearly to have conceived of the wind and rain as a kind of naughty child who can be got to behave properly by effacing the effects of its naughtiness.

We may notice something more in this early form of questioning. Children are apt to think not only that things behave in general after the manner of people, that their activity is motived by some aim, but that this aim concerns us human creatures. The wind and the rain came and went in our little girl's nature-theory just to vex and not to vex " mamma " and " Babba ". A little boy of two years two months sitting on the floor one day in a bad temper looked up and saw the sun shining and said captiously, "Sun not look at Hennie," and then more pleadingly, "Please, sun, not look at poor Hennie". Such observations show that children, like savages, and possibly, too, some persons who would not like to be called savages, are inclined to look at nature's doings as specially designed to injure or benefit themselves.

There is reason to think that the idea of use is prominent in the first conceptions of things. A French inquirer, M. Binet, has brought this fact out by questioning a considerable number of children. Thus, when asked what a hat is, one child answered, "Pour mettre sur la tête". Similarly children asked by other inquirers, "What is a tree?" answered, "To make the wind blow," "To sit under," and so forth.

Later on a more scientific form of questioning arises. The little searcher begins to understand something about the processes of nature, and tries by questioning his elders to get a glimpse into their manner of working. This quest of a natural explanation of things marks the transition to the level of thought of the civilised man.

Here, again, the small investigator finds much hard work to be got through, for nature's doings are apt to be varied and rather complex. A child, for example, finds that when he dips his hand into sand, clay, or what not, he makes a hole. But when he puts it into water no hole is left behind. Hence we can understand one little fellow asking his father, "How *is* it that when we put our hand into the water we don't make a hole in it?"

Here we have not mere curiosity; we have perplexity at what looks contradictory to the usual run

of things.   The same thing is illustrated in the question of another little boy, "Can they (the fish) breathe
with their moufs under water?"

Among the things which are apt to puzzle the
young inquirer is the disappearance of things.   He
can as little understand this as the beginning of things,
and so he will ask : "Where does the sea swim to?"
or "Where does the wind go to?" or "Where does
the wet (e.g., on the pavement after rain) go to?".

As the view of things begins to widen and embrace
the absent and the past new puzzles occur and
prompt to a more philosophical kind of questioning.
Sometimes it is the mere vastness of the world, the
multitude of things, which oppresses and confuses the
young understanding.   "Mother," asked a small boy
of four, "why is there such a lot of things in the
world if no one knows all these things?"   A little
girl about three and a half years old asked her
mother, "Mamma, why do there be any more days,
why do there? and why don't we leave off eating and
drinking?"   It is hard for us older folk to get behind
questions like this so as to understand the source of
the childish bewilderment.

The subject of origins is, as we all know, apt to be
a sore puzzle for the childish mind.   The beginnings
of living things are, of course, the great mystery.
"There's such a lot of things," remarked the little
zoologist I have recently been quoting, "I want to
know, that you say nobody knows, mamma.   I want
to know who made God, and I want to know if pussy
has eggs to help her make ickle (little) kitties."
Finding that this was not so, he observed : "Oh,
then, I s'pose she has to have God to help her if she

doesn't have kitties in eggs given her to sit on".
Another little boy, five years old, found his way to
the puzzle of the reciprocal genetic relation of the hen
and the egg, and asked his. mother : "When there *is*
no egg where does the hen come from? When there
was no egg, I mean, where *did* the hen come from ?"
Another little fellow was puzzled to know how the
first child was suckled, or, as a little girl of four and
a half years put it : " When everybody was a baby—
then who could be their nurse—if they were all babies?"

In this bold sweep of inquiry a child is apt to go
back to the absolute beginnings of things, as when he
asks, "Who made God ? " or, " What was there before
God ? " The idea that God has *always* been seems
to be particularly perplexing and even oppressive to
a child's mind.

Sometimes the questioning takes on a still clearer
ring of metaphysics, startling and shocking perhaps
the patient listener. A little boy of three once put
the poser : " If I'd gone upstairs, could God make it
that I hadn't ? " Or as another boy of eight put it
to a distinguished biologist, " Mr. —, Mr. —, if God
wanted me to be good, and I wouldn't be good, who
would win ? " Needless to say that this young philosopher was a Britisher.

With many children confronted with the mysteries
of God and the devil this questioning often reproduces
the directions of theological speculation. Thus the
problem of the necessity of evil is clearly recognisable
in the question once put by an American boy under
eight years of age to a priest who visited his home :
" Father, why don't God kill the devil and then there
would be no more wickedness in the world ? "

The different lines of questioning here briefly illustrated are apt to run on concurrently from about the end of the third year, a fit of eager curiosity about animals or other natural objects giving place to a fit of theological inquiry, this again being dropped for an equally eager inquiry into the making of clocks, railway engines, and so on.   Yet, through these alternating bouts of questioning we can recognise laws of progress.   Thus children will ask first about the things which first interest them, as, for example, animals and babies.   Again the questioning grows gradually more intelligent, more reasonable, accommodating itself, often after much suffering, to the adamantine limits of human knowledge.

While I have here regarded children's questioning seriously as the expression of a genuine desire for knowledge, I am well aware that this cannot be said of all of it.   The hard-pressed mother knows that a child's "why?" is often used in a sleepy mechanical way with no real desire for knowledge, any semblance of answer being accepted without an attempt to put a meaning into it.   A good deal of the more reckless kind of children's asking, when one question is followed by another with an irritating pertinacity, appears to be of this formal and lifeless character. Some of it, indeed, as when a little American asked her mother: "Mamma, why ain't Edna Belle (her baby sister) me, and why ain't I Edna Belle?" comes alarmingly near the rage of questioning observed in certain forms of mental disease, and may perhaps be a symptom of an over-wrought brain.

To admit this, however, is far from saying that we ought to treat all this questioning with a mild contempt. The little questioners flatter us by attributing superior knowledge to us, and good manners should compel us to treat their questions with some attention. And if now and then they torment us with a string of random reckless questioning, in how many cases, one wonders, are they not made to suffer, and that wrong-fully, by having perfectly serious questions rudely cast back on their hands?

CHAPTER V.

WE have seen in the last chapter that children have their characteristic ways of looking at their new world. These ways often result in the formation of definite ideas or "thoughts" which may last for years. We will now try to follow the little thinker in his first attempt at framing a theory of Nature and her doings.

Here, too, we shall find that the active little brain has its work cut out for it. As already suggested, things are often so puzzling to the child that it is only by dint of a good deal of questioning that he can piece them together at all. And even after he has had his questions answered he sometimes finds it well-nigh impossible to reconcile one fact with another, and to reach a clear view of things as a whole.

The Fashion of Things.

The first thoughts on Nature and her processes are moulded very largely by the tendencies of the young mind touched on in the last chapter. Like the savage the child is apt to think of the wind and the thunder as somebody's doing, and as aimed specially at himself. Hence the strongly marked mythological or super-natural element in children's theories. Here, it is

evident, thought is supported by a somewhat capricious fancy.   When, for example, a child accounts
for the wind by saying that somebody is waving a
very big fan somewhere, or, more prettily, that it is
made by the fanning of the angels' wings, he comes
very near that romancing which we have regarded as
the play of imagination. Yet though fanciful it is
still thought, just because it aims, however wildly, at
explaining something in the real world.

With this fanciful and mythological element there
goes a more scientific one.   Even the fan myth recognises a mechanical process, *viz.*, the waving of
something to and fro, which does undoubtedly produce a movement of the air.   Children's first theories
of nature often show a queer mingling of supernatural
and natural conceptions.

I propose now to examine a few of the commoner
ideas of children respecting natural objects.

One characteristic of this first thought about things
appears at an early age.   A child seems inclined to
take all that he sees for real tangible substance : it is
some time before he learns that "things are not what
they seem ".   For example, an infant will try to touch
shadows, sunlight dancing on the wall and flat objects
in pictures.   This tendency to make things out of all
he sees shows itself in pretty forms, as when a little girl
one year eleven months old, " gathered sunlight in her
hands and put it on her face," and about a month
earlier expressed a wish to wash some black smoke.
This was the same child that tried to make the wind
behave by tidying her mother's hair ; and her belief
in the material reality of the wind was shown by her
asking her mother to lift her up high so that she

might see the wind; which reminds one of R. L. Stevenson's lines to the wind :—

> I felt you push, I heard you call,
> I could not see yourself at all.

In making a reality out of the wind a child is led not by sight, but by touch.   He *feels* the wind, and so the wind must be something substantial.

The common childish thought about the wind shows that the young mind is apt to be much impressed by the movements of things.   Movement seems for all of us the clearest and most impressive manifestation of life.   When the movement of an object is not seen to be caused by some other object, but seems to be spontaneous, it is apt to be taken by children as by uncivilised races to be the sign of life, and of something like human impulse.   A child of eighteen months used to throw kisses to the fire.   Some children in the infant department of a London Board School were asked what things in the room were alive, and they promptly replied : " The smoke and the fire ". Big things moving by some internal contrivance of which the child knows nothing, more especially engines, are of course endowed with life.   A little girl of thirteen months offered a biscuit to a steam-tram, and the author of *The Invisible Playmate* tells us that his little girl wanted to stroke the " dear head " of a locomotive.

Next to movement a sound which seems to be produced by the thing itself leads children to endow it with life.   Are not movement and vocal sound the two great channels by which the child itself expresses its feelings and impulses?   The wind often owes something of its life to its sound. The common tendency of children to think of the sea as alive, of which M. Pierre Loti gives an excellent illustration in his *Roman d'un enfant,* is no doubt based on the perception of its noise and movement. A little boy assured his teacher that the wind was alive, for he heard it whistling in the night. The impulse, too, to endow with life an object which looks so very much of a machine as a railway engine, is probably supported by the knowledge of its puffing and whistling.

Closely related to this impulse to ascribe life to what we call inanimate objects is the tendency to conceive of them as growing. This is illustrated in the remark of a little boy of three and a half years who when criticised by his mother for trying to make a walking-stick out of a very short stick, observed : " Me use it for walking-stick when stick be bigger ".

I have referred in the last chapter to children's way of thinking of things as made by somebody. The idea of hand-work is extended in odd ways. For example, quite young children are apt to extend the ideas broken and mended to all kinds of objects. Anything which seems to have become reduced by losing a portion of itself is said to be " broken ". Thus a little boy of three, on seeing the moon partly covered by a cloud, remarked : "The moon is broken ". On the other hand, in the case of one little boy, everything not broken or intact was said to be " mended ". Do children when they talk in this fashion really think that things are constantly undergoing repairs at the hand of some mysterious mechanic, or are they using their familiar terms figuratively in default of others ? It is hard to say.

5

Curious thoughts about Nature's processes arise later when the inquirer tries to make them intelligible to himself. Here the first mechanical conceptions of the wind deserve attention. An American child, asked what a tree was, answered oddly, " To make the wind blow ". A pupil of mine distinctly recalls that when a child he accounted for the wind at night by the swaying of two large elms which stood in front of the house not far from the windows of his bedroom. This putting of the cart before the horse is funny enough, yet it is perfectly natural. All the wind-making a child can observe, as in blowing with his mouth, waving a newspaper, and so forth, is effected by the movement of a material object.

The Bigger World.

With respect to distant objects, a child is of course freer to speculate, and, as we know, his ideas of the heavenly bodies are wont to be odd enough. His thoughts about these remote objects are rendered quainter by his inability to conceive of great distances.

Children naturally enough take this world to be what it looks to their uninstructed eyes. Thus the earth becomes a circular plain, and the sky a sort of inverted bowl placed upon it. Many children appear like the ancients to suppose that the sky and the heavenly bodies touch the earth somewhere, and could be reached by taking a long, long journey. Other and similar ideas are formed by some. Thus one little girl used on looking at the sky to fancy she was inside a blue balloon. The heavenly bodies are apt to be taken for flat discs.   The brother of the little girl just referred to took the sun to be a big kind of cask cover, which could be put on the round globe to make a " see-saw ".

When this first simple creed gets corrected, children go to work to put a meaning into what is told them by their instructors.   Thus they begin to speculate about the other side of the globe, and, as Mr. Barrie reminds us, are apt to fancy they can know about it by peeping down a well.   When religious instruction introduces the new region of heaven they are wont to localise it just above the sky, which to their thought forms its floor.   Some hard thinking is carried out by the young heads in the effort to reconcile the various things they learn about the celestial region.   Thus the sky is apt to be thought of as *thin*, probably by way of explaining the light of the stars and moon, which is supposed to shine through the sky-roof.   One American child ingeniously applied the idea of the thinness of the sky to explain the appearance of the moon when one part is bright and the other faintly illumined, supposing it to be half-way through a sort of semi-transparent curtain.   Others again prettily accounted for the waning of the moon to a crescent by saying it was half stuck or half "buttoned" into the sky.

Characteristic movements of childish thought show themselves in framing ideas of the making of the world.   The boy of four described by Mrs. Jardine thought that the stars were " cut out " first, and that then the little bits left over were all rolled into the moon.   Such an idea of cosmogony seems nonsense till one remembers the work of cutting out the finer figures in paper.

In much the same way children try to understand
the movements of the sun and other heavenly bodies
by help of the familiar movements of terrestrial objects.
Thus the sun was thought by American children to
fly, to be blown, perhaps like a soap-bubble or air-
ball, and, by a child with a more mechanical turn, to
roll, presumably as a hoop rolls, and so forth. Theological ideas, too, are pressed into the service of
childish explanation, as when the disappearance of
the sun is ascribed to God's pulling it up higher out
of sight, to his taking it into heaven and putting it to
bed, and the like.

The impressive phenomena of thunder and lightning
give rise in the case of the child as in that of the
Nature-man to some fine myth-making. The American children, as already observed, have different
mechanical illustrations for describing the supernatural operation here, thunder being thought of as
the noise made by God when groaning, when walking
heavily on the floor of heaven, when he has coals " run
in "—ideas which show how naïvely the child-mind
humanises the Deity, making him a respectable citizen
with a house and a coal-cellar. In like manner the
lightning is attributed to God's lighting the gas, or
striking many matches at once. By a similar use of
familiar household operations God is supposed to
cause rain by turning on a tap, or by letting it down
from a cistern by a hose, or, better, by passing it
through a sieve or a dipper with holes.[1]

Throughout the whole region of these mysterious
phenomena we have illustrations of the tendency to

[1] I am indebted for these illustrations to an article by Dr. Stanley
Hall on " The Contents of Children's Minds ".

regard what takes place as designed for us poor mortals. Thus one of the American children referred to said charmingly that the moon comes round when people forget to light the lamps. The little girl of whom Mr. Canton writes thought "the wind and the rain and the moon 'walking' came out to see *her*, and the flowers woke up with the same laudable object". When frightened by the crash of the thunder a child instinctively thinks that it is all done to vex his little soul. An earthquake may be thought of as a kind of wonder show, specially got up for the admiration of a sufficient body of spectators. Two children, D. and K., aged ten and five respectively, lived in a small American town. D., who was reading about an earthquake, addressed his mother thus : "Oh, isn't it dreadful, mamma? Do you suppose we will ever have one here?" K., intervening with the character-istic impulse of the young child to correct his elders, answered : "Why, no, D., they don't have earthquakes in little towns like this". Later on Nature's arrange-ments are criticised from the same point of view. A girl of seven, going back to the interesting question of babies, remarked to her mother : "Wouldn't it be convenient if you laid an egg, and then if you changed your mind you needn't hatch it?"

Dreams.

Children are apt to have their own thoughts about the strange semblances of objects which sometimes present themselves to their eyes, more particularly the "spectra" which we see after looking at the sun or when the circulation of the retina is disturbed.

One little fellow spun quite a romance about the spectra he used to see when poorly, saying that they were angels, and that they went into his toy-basket and played with his toys.

The most common form of such illusory appearance is, of course, the dream, and I believe that children dwell much on the mystery of dreaming. The simpler kind of child, like the savage, is disposed to take his dreams for sensible realities. A boy in an elementary school in London, aged five years, said one day: "Teacher, I saw an old woman one night against my bed". Another child, a little girl in the same school, told her mother that she had seen a funeral last night, and on being asked, "Where?" answered quaintly, "I saw it in my pillow". A little boy whom I know once asked his mother not to put him to bed in a certain room, "because there were so many dreams in the room".

Yet children who reflect soon find out that dream-objects do not belong to the common world, in the sights of which we all partake. Another theory has then to be found. I believe that many children, especially those who, being imaginative when awake, make their fairy-stories and their own romancings very real to themselves, and who, as a result of this, are wont to return to them in their dreams, are inclined to identify dreamland and fairyland. If they want to see their "fairies" by day they will shut their eyes; and so the idea may naturally enough occur to them that when closing their eyes for sleep they are going to see the beloved fairies again, and for a longer time. Other ideas about dreams also occur among children. A gentleman tells me that when a child he used to think that dreaming, though different from actual seeing, was yet more than having one's own individual fancies ; on dreaming, for example, that he had met certain people he supposed that each of these must have had a dream in which he had met him. This, it may be remembered, is very much the fanciful idea of dreaming which Mr. Du Maurier works out in his pretty story *Peter Ibbetson.*

There is some evidence to show that a thoughtful child, when he begins to grasp the truth that dreams are only unreal phantasms, becomes confused, and wonders whether the things too which we see when waking are not unreal. Here is a quaint example of this transference of childish doubt from dreamland to the every-day world. A little boy five years old asked his teacher : "Wouldn't it be funny if we were dreaming?" and being satisfied by the reply elicited that it would be funny, he continued more explicitly : " Supposing every one in the whole world were dreaming, wouldn't *that* be funny ? They might be, mightn't they?" Receiving a slightly encouraging, "Perhaps they might," he wound up his argument in this fashion : "Yes, but I don't think we are—I'm sure we are not. Perhaps we should wake up and find *every one* gone away." This is dark enough, but suggests, I think, that doubt as to the bright beautiful forms seen in sleep is casting its shadow on the real world, on the precious certainty of the presence of those we love. A little girl about six and a half years old being instructed by her father as to the making of the world remarked : "Perhaps the world's a fancy". The doubt in this case too was, one may conjecture, led up to by the loss of faith in dreamland.

Birth and Growth.

We may now pass to some of children's character-istic thoughts about living things, more particularly human beings, and the familiar domestic animals. The most interesting of these, I think, are those respecting growth and birth.

As already mentioned, the growth of things is one of the most stimulating of childish puzzles. Led no doubt by what others tell him, a child finds that things are in general made bigger by additions from without, and his earliest conception of growth is, I think, that of such addition. Thus, plants are made to grow, that is, swell out, by the rain. The idea that the growth or expansion of animals comes from eating is easily reached by the childish intelligence, and, as we know, nurses and parents have a way of recommending the less attractive sorts of diet by telling children that they will make them grow. The idea that the sun makes us grow, often suggested by parents (who may be ignorant of the fact that growth *is* more rapid in the summer than in the winter), is probably interpreted by the analogy of an infusion of something into the body.

A number of children, I have found, have the queer notion that towards the end of life there is a process of shrinkage. Old people are supposed to become little again. One of the American children referred to, a little girl of three, once said to her mother: "When I am a big girl and you are a little girl I shall whip you just as you whipped me now". At first one is almost disposed to think that this child must have heard of Mr. Anstey's amusing story,

Vice Versâ. Yet I have collected a number of similar observations. For example, a little boy that I know, when about three and a half years old, used often to say to his mother with perfect seriousness of manner: " When I am big then you will be little, then I will carry you about and dress you and put you to sleep ". And one little girl asked about some old person of her acquaintance, " When will she begin to get small ? " Another little girl asked her grown-up cousin who was reading to her something about an old woman : " Do people turn back into babies when they get quite old ? "

Another interesting fact to be noted here is that some children firmly believe that persons after dying and going to heaven will return to earth as little children. An American lady writes to me that two of her boys found their way independently of each other to this idea. Thus one of them speaking of a playmate who had been drowned, and who was now, he was told, in heaven, remarked : " Then God will let him come back and be a baby again ".

What, it may be asked, is the explanation of this quaint childish thought? I think it probable that it is suggested in different ways. One must remember that as a child grows taller grown-ups may seem *by com-parison* to get shorter. Again old people are wont to stoop and so to look shorter; and then children often hear in their stories of " little old " people. I suspect, however, that in some cases there is a more subtle train of thought. As the belief of the two brothers in people's coming back from heaven suggests, the idea of shrinkage is connected with those of birth and death. May it not be that the more thoughtful sort of child reasons in this way? Babies which are sent from heaven must have been something there; and people when they die must continue to be something in heaven. Why, then, the "dead" people that go to this place are the very same as the babies that come from it. To make this theory "square" with other knowledge, the idea of shrinkage, either before or after death, has to be called in. That it takes place before death is supported by what was said above, and probably also by the information often given to children that people when they die are carried by angels to heaven just as the babies are said to be brought down to earth by the angels.

The origin of babies and young animals furnishes the small brain, as we have seen, with much food for speculation. Here the little thinker is not often left to excogitate a theory for himself. His inconvenient questionings in this direction have to be firmly checked, and thus arise the well-known legends about the doctor, the angel and so forth. With the various lore thus collected, supplemented by the pretty conceits of Hans Andersen and other writers of fairy stories, the young inquirer has to do his best.

How the child-thinker is apt to go to work here is illustrated in a collection of the thoughts of American school-children. Some of these said that God drops babies for the women and doctors to catch them, others that he brings them down to earth by means of a wooden ladder, others again, that mamma, nurse, or doctor goes up and fetches them in a balloon. They are said by other children to grow in cabbages, or to be placed by God in water, perhaps in the sewer, where they are found by the doctor, who takes them to sick folks that want them. Here we have delicious touches of childish fancy, quaint adaptations of fairy and Bible lore, as in the use of Jacob's ladder and the legend of Moses placed among the bulrushes, this last being enriched by the thorough master-stroke of child-genius, the idea of the dark, mysterious, wonder-producing sewer.

Not all children, by any means, elaborate even this crude sort of theory. The less speculative and more practical kind of child accepts what he is told and proceeds to apply it, sometimes oddly enough. Thus the *Lancet* recently contained an amusing letter from some children, the eldest of whom was seven, addressed to a doctor asking for a baby for their mother's next birthday. It was to be "fat and bonny, with blue eyes and fair hair"—a perfect doll in fact ; and a characteristic postscript asked: "Which would be the cheaper—a boy or a girl ? "

These ideas of children about babies partly communicated by others, partly thought out for themselves, are naturally enough made to account for the beginnings of animal life. This is illustrated in the supposition of the little boy, already quoted, who thought that God helps pussy to have "'ickle kitties," seeing that she hasn't any kitties in eggs given her to sit upon.

CHAPTER VI.

WE may now pass to some of the characteristic modes of child-thought about that standing mystery, the self. As our discussion of the child's ideas of origin, growth and final shrinkage suggests, a good deal of his most earnest thinking is devoted to problems relating to himself.

The Visible Self.

The date of the first thought about self, of the first dim stage of self-awareness, probably varies considerably in the case of different children according to the rapidity of the mental development and to the character of the surrounding circumstances. The little girl, who was afterwards to be known as George Sand, may be supposed to have had an exceptional development; and the blow which she received as a baby in arms, and to which she ascribes the first dawn of self-consciousness, was, of course, exceptional too. There are probably many robust and unreflective children, knowing little of life's misery, who get on extremely well without any consciousness of self.

The earliest idea of children about "myself" is a mental picture of the body. They come to learn that their body is different from other objects of sense by a number of experiences, such as grasping the foot, striking the head, receiving soft caresses, kisses, and so forth. Such experiences may suffice to develop even during the first year the idea that their body is "me" in the sense that it is the living seat of pain and pleasure.

The moving limbs are, of course, a specially interesting part of this bodily self. Yet there is reason to think that children regard the trunk as the most important and vital part of themselves. Thus one small boy who, when put to bed, could not get into a comfortable posture, said queerly: "I can't get my hands out of the way of myself". This may be because they learn to connect the impressive experiences of aches and pains with the trunk, and because they observe that the maimed can do without arms and without legs. It is interesting to note that in the development of the idea of the soul by the race its seat was placed in the trunk, *viz.*, the heart, long before it was localised in the head. Children are probably confirmed in this view of the supreme importance of the trunk by our way of specially referring to it when speaking of the "body".

About this interesting trunk-body, what is inside it, and how it works, the child speculates vastly. The experience of bleeding has suggested to some children that it is filled with blood. When later on the young thinker hears of the stomach, bones and so forth, he sets about theorising on these mysterious matters. Odd twistings of thought occur when the higher anatomy is talked of in his hearing. A six-year-old girl, of whom Mr. Canton writes, thus delivered herself with respect to the brain and its functions: "Brain is what you think with in your head, and the more you think the more crinkles there are". The growth of the folds was understood, with charming childish simplicity, as the immediate effect of thought, like the crinkling of the skin of the forehead.

At a later stage of the child's development, no doubt, when he begins to grasp the idea of a conscious thinking " I," the head will become a principal portion of the bodily self. Children are quite capable of finding their way, in part at least, to the idea that the mind has its lodgment in the head. But it is long before this thought grows clear. This may be seen in children's talk, as when a girl of four spoke of her dolly as having no sense in her *eyes.* Even after a child has learned from others that we think with our brains he may go on supposing that our thoughts travel down to the mouth when we speak.

Very interesting in connection with the first stages of development of the idea of self is the experience of the mirror. It would be absurd to expect a child when first placed before a glass to recognise his own face. He will smile at the reflection as early as the tenth week, though this is probably merely an expression of pleasure at the sight of a bright object. If held when about six months old in somebody's arms before a glass a baby will at once show that he recognises the image of the familiar face of his carrier by turning round to the real face, whereas he does not recognise his own. He appears at first and for some months to take it for a real object, sometimes smiling to it as to a stranger and even kissing it, or, as in the case of a little girl (fifteen months old), offering it things.

An infant will, we know, take a shadow to be a real object and try to touch it. Some children on noticing their own and other people's shadows on the wall are afraid as at something uncanny. Here, too, in time, as with young animals, *e.g.*, kittens, the strange appearance is taken as a matter of course.

Some children seem to follow out in part the line of thought of uncivilised races, and take reflections and shadows for a kind of "double" of the self. One of Dr. Stanley Hall's correspondents writes to him that he used to have small panics at his own shadow, trying to run away from it, and to stamp on it, thinking it might be his soul. We find another illustration of this doubling of the self in the auto-biography of George Sand, which relates that when a child, reflecting on the impressive experience of the echo, she invented a theory of her double existence. We know, too, that the boy Hartley Coleridge dis-tinguished among the " Hartleys " a picture Hartley and a shadow Hartley. To one little boy the idea of being photographed seemed uncanny, as if it were a robbing himself of something and the making of another self. But much more needs to be known about these matters.

The prominence of the bodily element in a child's first idea of himself is seen in the tendency to regard his sameness as limited by unaltered bodily appear-ance. A child of six, with his shock of curls, will, naturally enough, refuse to believe that he is the same as the hairless baby whose photograph the mother shows him. One boy who had attained to the dignity of knickerbockers used to speak of his petticoated predecessor as a little girl.

The Hidden Self.

In process of time, however, what we call the conscious self, that which thinks and suffers and wills, comes to be dimly discerned. It is probable that a real advance towards this true self-consciousness takes place towards the end of the third year, when the difficult forms of language, " I," " me," " mine," commonly come to be used with intelligence. This is borne out by the following story: A little girl of three lying in bed shut her eyes and said: "Mother, you can't see me now". The mother replied: "Oh, you little goose, I can see you but you can't see me". To which she rejoined: " Oh, yes, I know you can see *my body*, mother, but you can't see *me*". The " me " here was, I suppose, the expression of the inner self through the eyes. The same child at about the same age was concerned as to the reality of her own existence. One day playing with her dolls she asked her mother: " Mother, am *I* real, or only a pretend like my dolls ? "

The first thought about self as something existing apart from all that is seen is apt to be very perplexing to the thoughtful child. As one lady puts it, writing to me of her childish experience: " The power of feeling and acting and moving about myself, under the guidance of some internal self, amazed me continually ".

As may be seen by this quotation, the first thought about self is greatly occupied with its action on the body. Among the many things that puzzled one much-questioning little lad already quoted was this : " How do my thoughts come down from my brain to my mouth : and how does my spirit make my legs walk ? " A girl in her fifth year wanted to know how it is we can move our arm and keep it still when we want to, while the curtain can't move except somebody moves it.

The Unreachable Past.

Very curious are the directions of the first thought about the past self. The idea of what we call personal identity does not appear to be fully reached at first ; the little boy already quoted who referred to his past self by saying, "when I was a little girl," must have had a very hazy idea of his sameness with that small petticoated person. It would seem, indeed, as if a child found it easy to dissociate his present self from his past, to deny all kinship with it.

The difficulty to the child of conceiving of his remote past, is surpassed by that of trying to understand the state of things before he was born. The true mystery of birth for the child, the mystery which fascinates and holds his mind, is that of his beginning to be. This is illustrated in the question of a little boy : " Where was I a hundred years ago ? Where was I before I was born ? " It remains a mystery for all of us, only that after a time we are wont to put it aside.

Even when a child begins to take in the fact that there was a time when he was not, he is unable to think of absolute non-existence. A little girl of three

6

being shown a photograph of her family and not seeing her own face in the group asked : " Where is me ? " Being duly instructed that she was not here, or indeed anywhere, she asked : " Was I killed ? "

It is curious to note the differences in the attitude of children's minds towards this mystery, " before you were born ". A child accustomed to be made the centre of others' interest may be struck with the blank in the common home life before his arrival. A little girl of three, on being told by her mother of something which happened long before she was born, asked in amazement: "And what did you do without H. ? Did you cry all day for her ? "

Sometimes again, in the more metaphysical sort of child, the puzzle relates to the past existence of the outer world. We have all been perplexed by the thought of the earth and sky, and other folk existing before we were, and going on to exist after we cease to be ; though here again we are apt to "get used " to the puzzle. Children may be deeply impressed with this apparent contradiction. Jean Ingelow in the interesting reminiscences of her childhood writes : " I went through a world of cogitation as to whether it was really true that anything had been and lived before I was there to see it ". A little boy of five who was rather given to saying "clever " things, was one day asked by a visitor, who thought to rebuke what she took to be his conceit: " Why, M., however did the world go round before you came into it ? " M. at once replied : " Why, it *didn't* go round. It only began five years ago." This child, too, had probably felt little Jean Ingelow's difficulty.

A child will sometimes try to escape from this

puzzle by way of the supernatural ideas already referred to. If of quick intelligence he will see in the legend of babies brought from heaven to earth a way of prolonging his existence backwards. The same little boy that was so concerned to know what his mother had done without him, happened one day to be passing a street pump with his mother, when he stopped and observed with perfect gravity: "There are no pumps in heaven where I came from". He had evidently worked out the idea of heaven-sent babies into a theory of pre-natal existence.

In thinking of their past, children have to encounter that terrible mystery, time. They seem at first quite unable to think of time as we think of it, in an abstract way. "To-day," "to-morrow" and "yesterday" are spoken of as things which move. A girl of four asked: "Where is yesterday gone to?" and "Where will to-morrow come from?"

Another difficulty is the grasping of great lengths of time. A child is apt to exaggerate greatly a short period. The first morning at school has seemed an eternity to some who have carried the recollection of it into middle life. Even the minutes when, as Mrs. Maynell writes, "your mother's visitor held you so long at his knee, while he talked to her the excited gabble of the grown-up," may have seemed very, very big. Possibly this sense of the immeasurable length of certain experiences of childhood gives to the child's sense of past time something of an aching vastness which older people can hardly understand. Do not the words "long, long ago," when we use them in telling a child a story, still carry with them for our ears a strangely far-off sound?

Again, children find it hard to map out the divisions of time, and to see the relations of one period to another. One little boy about five and a half-finding that something had happened before his father was born, asked whether it was in the time of the Romans. His historical perspective had, not unnaturally perhaps, set the "time of the Romans" just before the life of the oldest of his household.

The Supernatural World.

A child's first acquaintance with the supernatural is frequently made through the medium of fairy-story or other fiction. And, as has been suggested in an earlier chapter, he can put a germ of thought into the tradition of a fairy-world. It is, however, when something in the shape of theological instruction supervenes that the supernatural becomes a problem for the young intellect. He is told of these mysterious things as of certainties, and in the measure in which he is a thinker, he will try to get a clear intelligent view of things.

Like the beginning of life, its ending is one of the recurring puzzles of early days. A child appears better able to imagine others dying than himself; this seems to be suggested by a story published by Stanley Hall of a little girl who from six to nine feared that all other people would die one by one, and that she would be left alone on the earth.

The first recoil from an inscrutable mystery soon begins to give place to a feeling of dread. A little girl of three and a half years asked her mother to put a great stone on her head, because she did not want to die. She was asked how a stone would prevent it, and answered with perfect childish logic: " Because I shall not grow tall if you put a great stone on my head ; and people who grow tall get old and then die ".

The first way of regarding death seems to be as a temporary state like sleep, which it so closely resembles. A little boy of two and a half years, on hearing from his mother of the death of a lady friend, at once asked : " Will Mrs. P. still be dead when we go back to London ? "

The knowledge of burial gives a new and alarming turn to the child's thought. He now begins to speculate much about the grave. The instinctive tendency to carry over the idea of life and feeling to the buried body is illustrated in the request made by a little boy to his mother : "Don't put earth on my face when I am buried ".

In the case of children who pick up something of the orthodox creed the idea of going to heaven has somehow to be grasped and put side by side with that of burial. Here comes one of the hardest puzzles for the logical child. One boy tried to reconcile the story of heaven with the fact of burial, at first by assuming that the good people who went to heaven were not buried at all ; and later by supposing that the journey to heaven was somehow to be effected after burial and by way of the grave. Other devices for getting a consistent view of things are also hit upon. Some children have supposed that the *head* only passes into heaven, partly from taking the " body " to be the trunk only, and partly from a feeling that the head is the seat of the thinking mind.

The idea of dead people going to heaven is, as we know, pushed by the little brain to its logical consequences. Animals when they die are, naturally enough, supposed to go to heaven also.

The Great Maker.

Children seem disposed, apart from religious instruction, to form ideas of supernatural beings. Sometimes it is a dreadful person who exerts a malign influence on the child, sending him, for example, his pains in the stomach. In other cases it is a fairy-like being who is created into a mighty benefactor, and half-worshipped and prayed to in childish fashion.

Even when religious instruction supplies the form of the supernatural being the young thinker deals with this in his own original way. He has to understand the mysteries of God, Satan and the rest, and he can only understand them by shedding on them the light of homely terrestrial facts. Hence the undisguised materialism of the child's theology. According to Dr. Stanley Hall's inquiries into the thoughts of American children, God is apt to be imaged as a big, very strong man or giant. One child thought of him as a huge being with limbs spread all over the sky ; another, as so tall that he could stand with one foot on the ground, and touch the clouds. He is commonly supposed, in conformity with what is told him, to dwell just above the sky, which last, as we have seen, is thought of as a dividing floor, through the chinks of which we get glimmerings of the glory of the heaven above. But some children show more of their own thought in localising the Deity, placing him, for example, in one of the stars, or the moon, or lower down "upon the hill".

Differences in childish feeling, as well as in intelligence, reflect themselves in the first ideas about the divine dwelling-place. It seems commonly to be conceived of as a grand house or mansion. While, however, some children deck it out with all manner of lovely things, including a park, flowers, and birds, others give it a homelier character, thinking, for example, of doors and possible draughts, like a little girl who asked God "to mind and shut the door, because he (*i.e.*, grandpapa who had just died) can't stand the draughts". Some children, too, of a less exuberant fancy are disposed to think of heaven as by no means so satisfyingly lovely, and rather to shrink from a long wearisome stay in it.

While thus relegated to the sublime regions of the sky God is supposed to be doing things, and of course doing them for us, sending down rain and so forth. What seems to impress children most, especially boys, in the traditional account of God is his power of making things. He is emphatically the artificer, the " demiurgos," who not only has made the world, the stars, etc., but is still kept actively employed by human needs. According to some of the American school-children he fabricates all sorts of things from babies to money, and the angels work for him. The boy has a great admiration for the maker, and one small English boy once expressed this oddly by asking his mother whether a group of working men returning from their work were " gods ".

This admiration for superior power and skill favours the idea of God's omnipotence. This is amply illus- trated in children's spontaneous prayers, which ask for things, from fine weather on a coming holiday to a baby with curly hair and other lovely attributes, with all a child's naïve faith. Yet a critical attitude will sometimes be taken up towards this mystery of unlimited power. The more logical and speculative sort of child will now and then put a sceptical question to his elders on this subject. A boy of eight turned over the problem whether God could beat him in a foot-race if he were starter and judge and refused to let God start till he had reached the goal ; and he actually measured out the racecourse on a garden path and went through the part of running, afterwards sitting down and giving God time to run, and then pondering the possibility of his beating him.

The idea of God's omniscience, too, may come readily enough to a child accustomed to look up ad- miringly to the boundless knowledge of some human authority, say a clergyman. Yet I know of cases where the dogma of God's infinite knowledge provoked in the child's mind a sceptical attitude. One little fellow remarked on this subject rather profanely : " I know a 'ickle more than Kitty, and you know a 'ickle more than me ; and God knows a 'ickle more than you, I s'pose ; then he can't know so very much after all ".

Another of the divine attributes does undoubtedly shock the child's intelligence. While he is told that God has a special abode in heaven, he is told also that he is here, there and everywhere, and can see everything. More particularly the idea of being always watched is, I think, repugnant to sensitive and high-spirited children. An American lady, Miss Shinn, speaks of a little girl, who, on learning that she was under this constant surveillance, declared that she "would *not* be so tagged". An English boy of three, on being informed by his older sister that God can see and watch us while we cannot see him, thought awhile, and then in an apologetic tone said: " I'm very sorry, dear, I can't (b)elieve you".

When the idea is accepted odd devices are excogitated by the active little brain for making it intelligible. Thus one child thought of God as a very small person who could easily pass through the key-hole. The opposite idea of God's huge framework, illustrated above, is probably but another attempt to figure the conception of omnipresence. Curious conclusions too are sometimes drawn from the supposition. Thus a little girl of three years and nine months one day said to her mother in the abrupt childish manner: "Mr. C. (a gentleman she had known who had just died) is in this room". Her mother, naturally a good deal startled, answered: "Oh, no!" Whereupon the child resumed: "Yes, he is. You told me he is with God, and you told me God was everywhere; so as Mr. C. is with God, he must be in this room."

It might easily be supposed that the child's readiness to pray to God is inconsistent with what has just been said. Yet I think there is no real inconsistency. Children's idea of prayer appears commonly to be that of sending a message to some one at a distance. The epistolary manner noticeable in many prayers, especially at the beginning and the ending, seems to illustrate this. The mysterious whispering in which a prayer is often conveyed is, I suspect, supposed in some inscrutable fashion known only to the child to transmit itself to the divine ear.

Of the child's belief in God's goodness it is needless to say much. For these little worshippers he is emphatically the friend in need who is just as ready as he is able to help them out of every manner of difficulty, and who, if they only ask prettily, will send them all the nice things they long for. Yet, happy little optimists as they are inclined to be, they will now and again be saddened by doubt, and wonder why the nice things asked for don't come, and why the dear kind God allows them to suffer so much.

While a child is thus apt to think of God as nicer than the nicest gentleman visitor who is wont to bring toys and do wondrous things for his delectation, he commonly imports into his conception a touch of human caprice. Fear may readily suggest to a child who has had some orthodox instruction that the wind howling at night is the noise of God's anger, or that the thunder is due to a sudden determination of the Creator to shoot him dead. The sceptical child, again, who is by no means so rare, may early begin to wonder how God can be so good and yet allow men to kill animals, and allow Satan to do such a lot of wicked things.

One of the hardest puzzles set to a child by the common religious instruction is the doctrine of God's eternity. The idea of a vast, endless "for ever,"

whether past or future, seems to be positively over-
whelming to many young minds. The continual
frustration of the attempt to reach a resting-place in
a beginning or an end may bring on something of
mental giddiness. Hence the wearisome perplexities
of the first thoughts about God's past. The question,
"Who made God?" seems to be one to which all
inquiring young minds are led at a certain stage of
child-thought. When told that God has always been,
unchanging, and knowing no youth, he wants to get
behind this "always was," just as at an earlier stage
of his development he wanted to get behind the
barrier of the blue hills.

Other mysteries of the orthodox faith may under-
go a characteristic solution in the hard-working mind
of a child. A friend tells me that when a child he
was much puzzled by the doctrine of the Trinity.
He happened to be an only child, and so he was led
to put a meaning into it by likening it to his own
family group, in which the Holy Ghost had, rather
oddly, to take the place of the mother.

Thoughtful children by odd processes of early
logic are apt when interpreting the words and actions
of their teachers to endow God with surprising attributes. For example, a boy of four asked his aunt
one Sunday to tell him why God was so fond of
three-penny bits. Asked why he thought God had
this particular liking, he explained by saying that he
noticed that on Sunday morning people ask for a
three-penny bit "instead of" three pennies, and that
as they take it to church he supposed that they gave
it to God.

I have tried to show that the more thoughtful

children seek to put meaning into the communications about the unseen world which they are wont to receive from their elders. Perhaps these elders if they knew what is apt to go on in a child's mind would reconsider some of the answers which they give to the little questioner, and select with more care the truths which, as they flatter themselves, they are making so plain to their little ones.

CHAPTER VII.

THE BATTLE WITH FEARS: (a) THE ONSLAUGHT.

IT is often asked whether children have as lively, as intense feelings as their elders. Those emotions of childhood which are wont to break out into violent expression, such as angry disappointment and gladness, may not, it is said, be in themselves so intense as they look. In order to get more data for settling the question we must try to reach their less demonstrative feelings, those which they are apt to hide from view out of shame, or some other impulse. Of these none is more interesting than fear, and it so happens that a good deal of inquiry has of late been directed to this feeling.

That we must not expect too much knowledge here seems certain. Fear is one of the shyest of the young feelings. A little fellow of two coming out of his grandpapa's house one evening into the darkness with his mother, asked her: "Would you like to take hold of my hand, mammy?" His father took this to mean the beginning of boyish determination not to show fear. Still, with the help of observations of parents, and later confessions and descriptions of childish fear, we may be able to get some insight into the dark subject.

That fear is one of the characteristic feelings of children needs, one supposes, no proving. In spite of the wonderful stories of Horatio Nelson, and of their reflections in literature, *e.g.*, Mr. Barrie's "Sentimental Tommy," I entertain the gravest doubts as to the existence of a perfectly fearless child. Children differ enormously, and the same child differs enormously at different times in the intensity of his fear, but they all have the characteristic *disposition* to fear. It seems to belong to these wee, weakly things, brought face to face with a new strange world, to tremble. They are naturally timid, as all that is weak and ignorant in nature is apt to be timid.

I have said that fear is well marked in the child. Yet, though it is true that a state of " being afraid " when fully developed shows itself by unmistakable signs, there are many cases where it is by no means easy to say whether the child experiences the feeling. People are apt to think that every time a child starts it is feeling afraid of something, but as we shall presently see, being startled and really frightened are two experiences, which, though closely related, must be carefully distinguished. A child may, further, show a sort of æsthetic repugnance to certain sounds, such as those of a piano; to ugly forms, *e.g.*, a hunchback figure; to particular touches, such as that of fur or velvet, without having the full experience of fear. Observers of children are by no means careful to distinguish true fear from other feelings which resemble it.

Fear proper shows itself in such signs as these, in the stare, the grave look, the movement of turning away and hiding the face against the nurse's or mother's shoulder, or of covering it with the hands. In the severer forms, known as terror, it leads to trembling and to wild shrieking. Changes of colour also occur, the child's face turning white, or possibly in some cases red. When frightened by anything an older child will commonly run from the object of his fear, though the violence of the feeling may some- times paralyse the limbs and chain the would-be fugitive to the spot. This often happens, I fancy, with a sudden oncoming of dread at discovering one- self alone in the dark.

The Battery of Sounds.

As is well known, sudden and loud sounds, such as that of a door banging, will give a shock to an infant in the first weeks of life, which though not amounting to fear is its progenitor. A clearer manifestation occurs when a new and unfamiliar sound calls forth the grave look, the trembling lip, and possibly the fit of crying. Darwin noticed these in one of his own boys at the age of four and a half months, when he produced the new sound of a loud snoring.

It is not every new sound which is thus discon- certing to the little stranger. Sudden sharp sounds of any kind seem to be especially disliked, as those of a dog's bark. A little girl burst out crying on first hearing the sound of a baby rattle ; and she did the same two months later on accidentally ringing a hand bell. Children often show curious caprices in their objections to sounds. Thus a little girl when taken into the country at the age of nine months took a liking to most of the animals she saw, but on hearing the bleating of the sheep showed a distinct germ of fear by sheltering herself against her nurse's shoulder.

So disturbing are new sounds apt to be to the

young child that even musical ones are often disliked at first.   The first hearing of the tones of a piano has upset the comfort of many a child.   A child of five and a half months conceived a kind of horror for a banjo, and screamed if it were played or only touched.

Animals may show a similar dread of musical sounds. I took a young cat of about eight weeks into my lap and struck some chords not loudly on the piano. It got up, moved uneasily from side to side, then bolted to a corner of the room and seemed to try to get up the walls. Many dogs, too, certainly appear to be put out, if not to be made afraid, on hearing the music of a brass band.

Fear of nature's great sounds, more especially the wind and thunder, which is common among older children, owes its intensity not merely to their volume, which seems to surround and crush, but also to the mystery of their origin.   We should remember too that sounds are, for the child still more than for the adult, expressive of feeling and intention.   Hence religious ideas readily graft themselves on to the noisy utterances of wind and thunder.   Wind is conceived of, for example, as the blowing of God when angry, and thunder, as we have seen, as his snoring, and so forth.

I am far from saying that all children manifest this fear of sounds.   Many babies welcome the new and beautiful sounds of music with a joyous greeting. Even the awful thunder-storm may gladly excite and not frighten.   Children will sometimes get through the first months without this fear, and then develop it as late as the second year.

I think, then, that in these disturbing effects of sound we have to do with something more than a mere nervous shock or a start. They involve a rudiment of the feeling of uneasiness at what is unexpected and disturbing, and so may be said to be the beginning of true childish fears. This element of anxiety becomes more clearly marked where the sound is not only disturbing but mysterious, as when a toy emits a sound, or water produces a rushing noise in some hidden pipe.

There is another kind of disturbance which shows itself also in the first year, and has a certain analogy to the discomposing effect of sound. This is the feeling of bodily insecurity which appears very early when the child is awkwardly carried, or when in dandling it, it is let down back-foremost. One child in her fifth month was observed when carried to hold on to the nurse's dress as if for safety. And it has been noticed by more than one observer that on dandling a baby up and down in one's arms, it will on descending, that is when the support of the arms is being withdrawn, show signs of discontent in struggling movements. This is sometimes regarded as an inherited fear ; yet it seems possible that, like the jarring effect of noise on the young nerves, it is the result of a rude disturbance. A child accustomed to the support of its cradle, the floor, or somebody's lap, might be expected to be put out when the customary support is withdrawn wholly or partially. The sense of equilibrium is disturbed in this case.

Other senses, more particularly that of touch, may bring their disturbing elements, too. Many children have a strong repugnance to cold clammy things, such

7

as a cold moist hand, and what seems stranger, to the touch of something that seems altogether so likable as fur. Whether the common dislike of children to water has anything to do with its soft yieldingness to touch I cannot say. This whole class of early repugnances to certain sensations seems to stand on the confines between mere dislikes and fears, properly so called. A child may very much dislike touching fur without being in the strict sense afraid of it, though the dislike may readily develop into a true fear.

The Alarmed Sentinel.

We may now pass to the disconcerting and alarming effects to which a child is exposed through his sense of sight. This, as we know, is the intellectual sense, the sentinel that guards the body, keeping a look-out for what is afar as for what is anear. The uneasiness which a child experiences at seeing things is not, like the uneasiness at sounds, a mere effect of violent sensation ; it arises much more from a perception of something menacing.

Among the earliest alarmers of sight may be mentioned the appearance of something new and strange, especially when it involves a sudden abolition of customary arrangements. Although we are wont to think of children as loving and delighting in what is new, we must not forget that it may also trouble and alarm. This feeling of uneasiness and apparently of insecurity in presence of changed surroundings shows itself as soon as a child has begun to grow used or accustomed to a particular state of things.

Among the more disconcerting effects of a rude departure from the customary, is that of change of place. When once an infant has grown accustomed to a certain room it is apt to find a new one strange, and will eye its features with a perceptibly anxious look. This sense of strangeness in places sometimes appears very early. A little girl on being taken at the age of four months into a new nursery, " looked all round and then burst out crying ". Some children retain this feeling of uneasiness up to the age of three years and later. Here, again, clearly marked differences among children disclose themselves. On entering an unfamiliar room a child may have his curiosity excited, or may be amused by the odd look of things, so that the fear-impulse is kept under by other and pleasanter ones.

What applies to places applies also to persons. A child may be said to combine the attachment of the dog to persons with that of the cat to localities. Any sudden change of the customary human surroundings,. for example, the arrival of a stranger on the scene, is apt to trouble him.

During the first three months, there is no distinct manifestation of a fear of strangers. It is only later, when recurring forms have grown familiar, that the approach of a stranger, especially if accompanied by a proposal to take the child, calls forth clear signs of displeasure and the shrinking away of fear. Professor Preyer gives between six and seven months as the date at which his boy began to cry at the sight of a strange face.

Here, too, curious differences soon begin to disclose themselves, some children showing themselves more hospitable than others. It would be curious to compare the ages at which children begin to take kindly to new faces. Professor Preyer gives nineteen months as the date at which his boy surmounted his timidity.

One strange variety of the fear of strangers is the uneasiness shown in presence of some one who is only partially recognisable. One little boy of eight months moaned in a curious way when his nurse returned home after a fortnight's holiday. Another boy of about ten months is said to have shown a marked shrinking from an uncle who strongly resembled his father. Such facts, taken with the familiar one that children are apt to be frightened at the sight of a parent partially disguised, suggest that half-stranger half-friend may be for a child's mind worse than altogether a stranger.

The uneasiness which comes from a sense of being in a new room or face to face with a stranger may perhaps be described as a feeling of what the Germans call the "unhomely". The little traveller has lost his bearings, and he begins to feel that he himself is lost. This effect of homelessness is, of course, most marked when a child finds himself in a strange place. Much of the acuter fear of children probably has in it something of this dizzy sickening sense of being lost. A little girl between the ages of seven and ten used to wake up in a fright crying loudly because she could not think where she was. Many a child when exploring a new and dark room, or still more venturesomely wandering alone out of doors, has suddenly woke up to the strange homeless look of things. I once saw a wee girl at a children's party who appeared to enjoy herself well enough up to a certain point, but was then suddenly seized by this sense of being lost in a new room among new faces, so that all her older sister's attempts to reassure her failed to stay the paroxysm of grief and terror.

We may see a measure of this same distrust of the new, this same clinging to the homely, in many of children's lesser fears, as, for example, that of new clothes. An infant has been known to break out into tears at the sight of a new dress on its mother, though the colour and pattern had, one would have supposed, nothing alarming. The fear of black clothes, of which there are many known examples, probably includes further a special dislike for this colour.

Here, again, we may see two opposed impulses at work, of which either one or the other may be uppermost in different children, or at different times in the same child. The dread of new clothes has its natural antagonist in the love of new clothes, which is often supported in children of a "subjective" turn by a feeling of something like disgrace at having to go on wearing the same clothes so long. Sometimes the love of novelty becomes a passion. The boy Alfred de Musset at the age of four, watching his mother fitting on his feet a pair of pretty red shoes, exclaimed : " Dépêche toi, maman, mes souliers neufs vont devenir vieux ".

Some other fears closely resemble that of new clothes insomuch as they involve an unpleasant transformation of a familiar object, the human figure, the mainstay of a child's trust. Possibly the alarming effect of making faces, which is said to disturb a child within the first three months, illustrates the effect of shock at the spoiling of what is getting familiar and liked. The donning of a pair of dark spectacles, by extinguishing the focus of childish interest, the eye, will produce a like effect of the uncanny. Children show a similar dislike and fear at the sight of an ugly doll with features greatly distorted from the familiar pattern.

The fear of certain big objects contains, I think, the germ of this feeling of uneasiness in the presence of strange surroundings. One of the best illustrations of this is produced by a first sight of the sea. Some children clearly show signs of alarm, nestling towards their nurses when they are carried near the edge of the water. Yet here, again, the behaviour of the childish mind varies greatly. A little boy who first saw the sea at the age of thirteen months exhibited signs not of fear but of wondering delight, prettily stretching out his tiny hands towards it as if wanting to go to it.

I am disposed to think that imaginative children, whose minds take in something of the bigness of the sea, are more susceptible of this variety of fear. This conjecture is borne out by the case of two sisters, of whom one, an imaginative child, had not even at the age of six got over her fear of going into the sea, whereas the sister, who was comparatively unimaginative, was perfectly fearless. The supposition finds a further confirmation in the descriptions given by imaginative writers of their early impressions of the sea, for example, that of M. Pierre Loti in his volume *Le Roman d'un Enfant*.

The fear of an eclipse of the moon and other celestial phenomena, owes something of its force and

persistence to their unknown and inaccessible character. A child is easily annoyed at that great white
thing, which seems like a human face to look down
on him, and which never comes a step nearer to let
him know what it really is. It may be conjectured
too that a child's fear of clouds, when they take on
uncanny forms, is supported by their inaccessibility ;
for he cannot get near them and touch them. It
seems, however, according to some recent researches
in America, that children's fear of celestial bodies,
especially the moon and clouds, is connected with the
thought that they may fall on them. The idea of
these strange-looking objects above the head, having
no visible support, and often taking on a threatening
mien, may well give rise to fear in a child's breast
akin to the superstitious fear of the savage.

Self-moving objects, which are not manifestly living
things, are apt to excite a feeling of alarm in children,
as indeed to some extent in the more intelligent
animals. Just as a dog will run away from a leaf
whirled about by the wind, so children are apt to be
terrified by the strange and quite irregular behaviour
of a feather as it glides along the floor or lifts itself
into the air. A girl of three, who happened to pull
a feather out of her mother's eider-down quilt, was so
alarmed at seeing it float in the air that she would
not come near the bed for days afterwards. Shrewd
nurses know of this weakness, and have been able
effectually to keep a child in a room by putting
a feather in the keyhole. The fear here seems to be
of something which simulates life and yet is not recognisable as a familiar living form. It was, I suppose,
the same uncanny suggestion of life which made a

child of four afraid at the sight of a leaf floating on the water of the bath-tub. Fear of feathers is, I believe, known among the superstitions of adults.

This simulation of life by what is perceived to be not alive probably takes part in other forms of childish dread. Toys which take on too impudently the appearance of life may excite fear, as, for example, a toy cow which "moved realistically when it reared its head," a combination which completely scared its possessor, a boy about the age of one and a half years. A child can itself *make* its toy alive, and so does not want the toy-maker to do so.

The fear of shadows, which appears among children as among superstitious adults, seems to arise partly from their blackness and eerie forms, partly from their uncanny movements and changes of form. Some of us can recall with R. L. Stevenson the childish horror of going up a staircase to bed when,

> . . . all round the candle the crooked shadows come,
> And go marching along up the stair.

One's own shadow is worst of all, doggedly pursuing, horribly close at every movement, undergoing all manner of ugly and weird transformations.

CHAPTER VIII.

THE BATTLE WITH FEARS (*Continued*).

The Assault of the Beasts.

THERE are two varieties of children's fears so prominent and so important that it seems worth while to deal with them separately. These are the dread of animals and of the dark.

It may well seem strange that the creatures which are to become the companions and playmates of children, and one of the chief sources of their happiness, should cause so much alarm when they first come on the scene. Yet so it is. Many children, at least, are at first terribly put out by quite harmless members of the animal family.

In some cases, no doubt, as when a child takes a strong dislike to a dog after having been alarmed at its barking, we have to do with the disturbing effect of sound merely. Fear here takes its rise in the experience of shock. In other cases we have to do rather with a sort of æsthetic dislike to what is disagreeable and ugly than with a true fear. Children sometimes appear to feel a repugnance to a black sheep or other animal just because they dislike black objects, though the feeling may not amount to fear properly so called.

Yet allowing for these sources of repugnance, it seems probable that many children from about two or three onwards manifest something indistinguishable from fear at the first sight of certain animals. The directions of this childish fear vary greatly. Darwin's boy when taken to the Zoological Gardens at the age of two years three months showed a fear of the big caged animals whose forms were strange to him, such, *e.g.*, as the lion and the tiger. Some children have shown fear on seeing a tame bear, others have selected the cow as their pet dread, others the butting ram, and so forth. Nor do they confine their aversions to the bigger animals. Snakes, caterpillars, worms, small birds such as sparrows, spiders and even moths have looked alarming enough to throw a child into a state of terror.

It is sometimes thought that these early fears of animals are inherited from remote ancestors to whom many wild animals were really dangerous. But I do not think that this has been proven The variety of these childish recoilings, and the fact that they seem to be just as often from small harmless creatures as from big and mighty ones, suggest that other causes are at work here. We may indeed suppose that a child's nervous system has been so put together and poised that it very readily responds to the impression of strange animal forms by a tremor. Special aspects of the unfamiliar animal, aided by special character-istics of its sounds, probably determine the direc-tions of this tremor.

In many cases, I think, the mere bigness of an animal, aided by the uncanny look which often comes from an apparent distortion of the familiar human face, may account for some of these early fears. In other cases we can see that it is the suggestion of attack which alarms. This applies pretty certainly to the butting ram, and may apply to pigeons and other birds whose pecking movements readily appear to a child's mind a kind of attack. And this supplies an explanation of the fear of one boy of two years three months at the sight of pigs when sucking ; for, as the child let out afterwards, he thought they were biting their mother. The unexpectedness of the animal's movements too, especially when, as in the case of birds, mice, spiders, they are rapid, might excite uneasiness. In other cases it is something uncanny in the movement which excites fear, as when one child was frightened at seeing a cat's tail move when the animal was asleep. The apparent fear of worms and caterpillars in some children may be explained in this way, though associations of disagreeable touch probably assist here. In the case of many of the smaller animals, *e.g.*, small birds, mice, and even insects when they come too near, the fear may not improbably have its source in a vague apprehension of invasion.

These shrinkings from animals are among the most capricious-looking of all childish fears. Many robust children with hardy nerves know little or nothing of them. Here, too, as in the case of new things generally, the painfulness of fear is opposed and may be overcome by the pleasure of watching and by the deeper pleasure of " making friends ". Quite tiny children, on first seeing ducks and other animals, so far from being alarmed, will run after the pretty creatures to make pets of them. Nothing perhaps is prettier in child-life than the pose and look of one of these defenceless youngsters when he is making a brave effort to get the better of his fear at the approach of a strange big dog and to proffer friendship to the shaggy monster. The perfect love which lies at the bottom of children's hearts towards their animal kinsfolk soon casts out fear. And when once the reconciliation has been effected it will take a good deal of harsh experience to make the child ever again entertain the thought of danger.

The Night Attack.

Fear of the dark, and especially of *being alone* in the dark, which includes not only the nocturnal dread of the dark bedroom, but that of closets, caves, woods, and other gloomy places, is no doubt very common among children. It does not show itself in the early months. A baby of three or four months if accustomed to a light may no doubt be upset at being deprived of it; but this is some way from a dread of the dark. This presupposes a certain development of the mind, and more particularly what we call imagination. It is said by Dr. Stanley Hall to attain its greatest strength about the age of five to seven, when images of things are known to be vivid.

So far as we can understand it the fear of the dark is rarely of the darkness as such. The blackness present to the eye in a dark room does no doubt encompass us and seem to close in upon and threaten to stifle us. We know, too, that children sometimes show fear of mists, and that many are haunted by the idea of the stifling grave. Hence, it is not improbable that children seized by the common terror and dizziness on suddenly waking may feel the darkness as something oppressive. This is borne out by the fact that a little boy on surmounting his dread told his father that he used to think the dark " a great large live thing the colour of black ". A child can easily make a substantial thing out of the dark, as he can out of a shadow.

Yet in most, if not all, cases imagination is active here. The darkness itself offers points for the play of imagination. Owing to the activity of the retina, which goes on even when no light excites it, brighter spots are apt to stand out from the black background, to take form and to move ; and all this supplies food to a child's fancy. I suspect that the alarming eyes of people and animals which children are apt to see in the dark receive their explanation in this way. Of course these sources of uneasiness grow more pronounced when a child is out of health and his nervous tone falls low. Even older people who have this fear describe the experience as seeing shadowy flitting forms, and this suggests that the activity of that wonderful little structure the retina is at the bottom of it. The same thing seems to be borne out by the common dread in the dark of *black* forms, *e.g.*, a black coach with headless coachman dressed in black. A girl of nineteen remembers that when a child she seemed on going to bed to see little black figures jumping about between the ceiling and the bed.

The more familiar forms of a dread of the dark are sustained by images of threatening creatures which lie hidden in the blackness or half betray their presence in the way just indicated. These images are in many cases the revival of those acquired from the experiences of the day, and from storyland. The fears of the day live on undisturbed in the dark hours of night. The dog that has frightened a child will, when he goes to bed, be projected into the surrounding blackness. Any shock in the waking hours may in this way give rise to a more or less permanent fear of being alone in a dark place. In not a few instances the alarming images are the product of fairy-stories, or of ghost and other alarming stories told by nurses and others thoughtlessly. In this way the dark room becomes for a timid child haunted by a "bogie" or other horror. Alarming animals, generally black, as that significant expression *bête noire* shows, are frequently the dread of these solitary hours in the dark room. Lions and wolves, monsters not describable except by saying that they have claws, which they can stretch out, these seem to fill the blackness for some children. The vague horrors of big black shapeless things are by no means the lightest to bear.

In addition to this overflow of the day's fears into the unlit hours, sleep and the transitional states between sleeping and waking also furnish much alarming material. Probably the worst moment of this trouble of the night is when the child wakes suddenly from a sleep or half-sleep with some powerful dream-image still holding him in its clutches, and when the awful struggle to wake and to be at home with the surroundings issues in the cry, "Where am I?" It is in these moments of absolute hopeless confusion that the impenetrable blackness, refusing to divulge its secret, grows insufferable. The dream-images, but slightly slackening their hold, people the blackness with nameless terrors. The little sufferer has to lie and battle with these as best he may, perhaps till the slow-moving day brings reassuring light and the familiar look of things.

How terrible beyond all description, all measurement with other things, these nightmare fears may be in the case of nervous children, the reminiscences of Charles Lamb and others have told us. It is not too much, I think, to say that to many a child this dread of the black night has been the worst of his sufferings. At no time is he really so brave as when he lies still in a cold damp terror and trusts to the coming of the morning light.

I do not believe that fear of the dark is universal among young children. I know a child that did not show any trace of it till some rather too gruesome stories of Grimm set his brain horror-spinning when he ought to have been going to sleep. A lady whom I know tells me that she never had the fear as a child though she acquired it later, towards the age of thirty. How common it is among children under ten or twelve, we have as yet no means of judging. Some inquiries of Dr. Stanley Hall show that out of about 300 young people under thirty only two appear to have been wholly exempt from. it, but the ages at which the fear first appeared are not given.

Here, again, we have a counterbalancing side. An imaginative child can fill the dark vacancy of the bedroom with bright pleasing images. On going to bed and saying good-night to the world of daylight, he can see his beloved fairies, talk to them and hear them talk. We know how R. L. Stevenson must, when a child, have gladdened many of his solitary dark hours by bright fancies. Even when there is a little trepidation a hardy child may manage to play with his fears, and so in a sense to enjoy his black phantasmagoria, just as grown-ups may enjoy the horrors of fiction.

It will perhaps turn out that imaginative children have both suffered and enjoyed the most in these ways, the effect varying with nervous tone and mental condition. Yet it seems probable that the fearful suffering mood has here been uppermost.

Why these nocturnal images tend to be gloomy and alarming may, I think, be explained by a number of circumstances. The absence of light and the on-coming of night have, as we know, a lowering effect on the functions of the body; and it is not unlikely that this might so modify the action of the brain as to favour the rise of gloomy thoughts. The very blackness of night, too, which we must remember is actually seen by the child, would probably tend to darken the young thoughts. We know how commonly we make black and dark shades of colour symbols of melancholy and sorrow. If to this we add that in the night a child is apt to feel lost through a loss of all his customary landmarks, and that, worst of all, he is, in the midst of this blackness which blots out his daily home, left to himself, robbed of that human companionship which is his necessary stay and comfort, we need not, I think, wonder at his so often encountering "the terror by night".

(b) Damage of the Onslaught.

I have now, perhaps, illustrated sufficiently some of the more common and characteristic fears of children. The facts seem to show that they are exposed on

different sides to the attacks of fear, and that the
attacking force is large and consists of a variety of
alarming shapes.

If now we glance back at these several childish
fears, one feature in them which at once arrests our
attention is the small part which remembered experiences of evil play in their production. The child is
inexperienced, and if humanely treated knows little of
the acuter forms of human suffering. It would seem
at least as if he feared not so much because his experience had made him aware of a real danger in this
and that direction, as because he was constitutionally
and instinctively nervous, and possessed with a feeling
of insecurity. More particularly children are apt to
feel uneasy when face to face with the new, the
strange, the unknown, and this uneasiness grows into
a more definite feeling of fear as soon as the least
suggestion of harmfulness is added ; as when a child
recoils with dread from a stranger who has a big
projecting eye that looks a menace, or a squint which
suggests a sly way of looking at you, or an ugly and
advancing tooth that threatens to bite. How much
the fear of the dark is due to inability to see and so
to know is shown by the familiar fact that children
and adults who can enter a strange gloomy-looking
room and keep brave as long as things are before
their eyes are wont to feel a creepy sense of "something" behind them when they turn their backs to retire and can no longer see. It is shown too in the
common practice of children and their elders to look
into the cupboard, under the bed, and so forth, before
putting out the light ; for that which has not been inspected retains dire possibilities of danger.

8

Where a child does not know he is apt to fancy something. It is the activity of children's imagination which creates and sustains the larger number of their fears. Do we not indeed in saying that they are for the greater part groundless say also that they are " fanciful " ?

Children's fears are often compared with those of animals. No doubt there are points of contact. The misery of a dog when street music is going on is very suggestive of a state of uneasiness if not of fully developed fear. Dogs, cats, and other animals will " shy " at the sight of " uncanny " moving objects, such as leaves, feathers, and shadows. Yet the great point of difference remains that animals not having imagination are exempt from many of the fearful foes which menace childhood, including that arch-foe, the black night.

A much more instructive comparison of children's fears may be made with those of savages. Both have a like feeling of insecurity in presence of the big unknown, especially the mysterious mighty things, such as the storm-wind, and the rare and startling things, *e.g.*, the eclipse and the thunder. The ignorance and simplicity of mind, moreover, aided by a fertile fancy, which lead to this and that form of childish fear are at work also in the case of uncivilised adults. Hence the familiar observation that children's superstitious fears often reflect those of savage tribes.

While children have this organic predisposition to fear, the sufferings introduced by what we call human experience begin at an early date to give definite direction to their fears. How much it does this in the first months of life it is difficult to say. In the aversion of a baby to its medicine glass, or its cold bath, one sees, perhaps, more of the rude germ of passion or anger than of fear. Some children, at least, have a surprising way of going through a good deal of physical suffering from falls, cuts and so forth, without acquiring a genuine fear of what hurts them. It is a noteworthy fact that a child will be more terrified during a first experience of pain, especially if there be a visible hurt and bleeding, than by any subsequent prospect of a renewal of the suffering.

Even where fear can be clearly traced to experience it is doubtful whether in all cases it springs out of a definite expectation of some particular kind of harm. When, for example, a child who has been frightened by a dog betrays signs of fear at the sight of a kennel, and even of a picture of a dog, may we not say that he dreads the sight and the idea of the dog rather than any harmful act of the animal?

In these fears, then, we seem to see much of the workmanship of Nature, who has so shaped the child's nervous system and delicately poised it that the trepidation of fear comes readily. According to some she has done more, burdening a child's spirit with germinal remains of the fears of far-off savage ancestors, to whom darkness and the sounds of wild beasts were fraught with danger. That, however, is far from being satisfactorily demonstrated. We can see why in the case of children, as in that of young animals, Nature tempers a bold curiosity of the new by mingling with it a certain amount of uneasiness, lest the ignorant helpless things should come to grief by wandering from parental shelter and supplies. This, it seems to me, is all that Nature has done.

And in so doing has she not, with excellent economy, done just enough?

The extent of suffering brought into child-life by the assaults of fear is hard to measure. Even the method of questioning young people about their fears, which is now in vogue, is not likely to bring us near a solution of this problem. And this for the good reason that children are never more reticent than when talking of their fears, and that by the time the fears are surmounted few can be trusted to give from memory an accurate report of them. One thing seems pretty clear, and the new questioning of children which is going on apace in America seems to bear it out, *viz.*, that, since it is the unknown which is the primary occasion of these childish fears, and since the unknown in childhood is almost everything, the possibilities of suffering from this source are great enough.

> Alike the Good, the Ill offend thy Sight,
> And rouse the stormy sense of shrill affright.

(c) *Recovery from the Onslaught.*

Nevertheless it is quite possible here to go from one extreme of indifference to another of sentimental exaggeration. Even allowing what George Sand says, that fear is "the greatest moral suffering of children," the suffering may turn out to be less cruelly severe than it looks.

To begin with, then, if children are sadly open to the attacks of fear on certain sides they are completely defended on other sides by their ignorance. This is well illustrated in the pretty story of the child Walter Scott, who was found out of doors lying on his back during a thunderstorm, clapping his hands and shouting, "Bonnie! bonnie!" at each new flash.

Again, if, as we have supposed, children's fears are mostly due to a feeling of insecurity in view of the unknown, they may be said to correct themselves to a large extent. By getting used to the disturbing sound, the ugly black doll, and so forth, a child, like a dog, tends to lose its first fear. One must say "tends," for the well-known fact that many persons carry with them into later life their early fear of the dark shows that when once the habit of fearing has got set no amount of familiarity will suffice to dissolve it.

Not only are the points of attack thus limited ; the attack when it does take place may bring something better than a debasing fear. A child may, it is certain, suffer acutely when it is frightened. But if only there is the magic circle of the mother's arms within reach may it not be said that the fear is more than counterbalanced by the greatest emotional luxury of childhood, the loving embrace? It is the shy fears, breeding the new fear of exposure to unloving eyes and possibly to ridicule, which are the tragedy of childhood.

In addition to these extraneous aids children are provided by Nature with capacities of self-defence. I have pointed out that the impulses of curiosity and fear lie close together in a child's mind, so that one can hardly say beforehand which of the two is going to be awakened first by the coming of the new and strange thing. The eager desire to know about things is perhaps the most perfect inward defence against many childish fears. Even when fear is half awake the passionate longing to see will force its way. A little girl that was frightened at a Japanese doll just given her and would not approach it, insisted on seeing it at some distance every day. The same backing of a timid child's spirit by hardy curiosity shows itself in his way of peeping at a dog which has just terrified him and gradually approaching the monster.

Better still, in the hardier race of children Nature has planted an impulse which not only disarms fear but turns it into a frolicsome companion. Many children, I feel sure, maintain a . double attitude towards their terrors, the bogies, the giants and the rest. Moments of cruel suffering alternate with moments of brave exultation. Fear in children, even more than in adults, is an instinctive process into which but little thought enters. If the nerves are slack, and if the circumstances are eerie and fear-provoking, the sudden strange sound, the appearance of a black something, will send the swift shudder through the small body; if, on the other hand, the child is cooler and has the cheering daylight to back him, he may be bold enough to play with his fears, and to talk of them to others with the chuckle of superiority.[1] The more real and oppressive the fit of fear the more enjoyable is the subsequent self-deliverance by a perspicacious laugh likely to be. The beginnings of childish bravery often take the form of laughing away their fears. Even when the ugly phantoms are not wholly driven back they are half seen through, and the child who is strong enough can

[1] Mrs. Meynell gives an example of this in her volume *The Children* (" The Man with Two Heads ").

amuse himself with them, suffering the momentary compression for the sake of the joyous expansion which so swiftly follows. A child of two, the same that asked his mother, "Would you like to take hold of my hand?" was once taken out by her on a little sledge. Being turned too suddenly he was pitched into the snow, almost on his head; but on being picked up by his mother he remarked quite calmly: "I nearly tumbled off". Another child of six on entering an empty room alone, stamped his foot and shouted: "Go away everything that's here!" In such ways do the nerves of a strong child recover themselves after shock and tremor, taking on something of the steady pose of human bravery.

CHAPTER IX.

GOOD AND BAD IN THE MAKING.

CHILDREN have had passed on their moral characteristics the extremes of human judgment. By some, including a number of theologians, they have been viewed as steeped in depravity; by others, *e.g.*, Rousseau, they have been regarded as the perfection of the Creator's workmanship.

If we are to throw any light on the point in dispute we must avoid the unfairness of applying grown-up standards to childish actions, and must expect neither the vices nor the virtues of manhood. We must further take some pains to get, so far as this is possible, at children's natural inclinations so as to see whether, and if so how far, they set in the direction of good or of bad.

Traces of the Brute.

Even a distant acquaintance with the first years of human life tells us that young children have much in common with the lower animals. The characteristic feelings and impulses are centred in self and the satisfaction of its wants. What is better marked, for example, than the boundless greed of the child, his keen desire to appropriate and enjoy whatever presents itself, and to resent others' participation in such enjoyment?

We note, further, that when later on he makes fuller acquaintance with his social surroundings, his first attitude has in it much of the hostility of the Ishmaelite. The removal of the feeding bottle before full satisfaction has been attained is, as we know, the occasion for one of the most impressive utterances of the baby's "will to live," and of its resentment of all human checks to its native impulses. Here we have the first rude germ of that opposition of will which makes the Ishmaelite look on others as his foes.

The same attitude of isolating hostility is apt to show itself towards other children. In the matter of toys, for example, the natural way of a child is very frequently not only to make free with other children's property when he has the chance, but to show the strongest objection to any imitation of this freedom by others, sometimes indeed to display a dog-in-the-manger spirit by refusing to lend what he himself does not want.

The same vigorous egoism inspires the whole scale of childish envies and jealousies, from those having to do with things of the appetite to those which trouble themselves about the marks of others' good-will, such as caresses and praises.

In this wide category of childish egoisms we seem to be near the level of animal ways. Out of all this fierce pushing of desire whereby the child comes into rude collision with others' wishes, there issue the storms of young passion. The energy of these displays of wrath as the imperious little will feels itself suddenly pulled up has in spite of its comicality something impressive. We all know the shocking scene as the boy Ishmaelite gives clearest and most emphatic utterance to his will by hitting out with his arms, stamping and kicking, throwing things down on the floor and breaking them, and accompanying this war-dance with savage howlings and yellings. The outburst tends to concentrate itself in a real attack on somebody. Sometimes this is the offender, as when Darwin's boy at the age of two years and three months would throw books, sticks, etc., at any one who offended him. But almost anybody or anything will do as an object of attack. A child of four on having his lordly purpose crossed would bang his chair, and then proceed to vent his displeasure on his unoffending toy lion, banging him, jumping on him, and, as anti-climax, threatening him with the loss of his dinner. Hitting is in many cases improved upon by biting.

Such fits of temper, as we call them, vary in their manner from child to child. Thus, whereas one little boy would savagely bite or roll on the floor, his sister was accustomed to dance about and stamp. They vary greatly too in their frequency and their force. Some children show in their anger little if anything of savage furiousness. It is to be added, that with those who do show it, it is wont in most cases to appear only for a limited period.

The resemblance of this fierce anger to the fury of the savage and of the brute can hardly fail to be noticed. Here indeed, as is illustrated in the good hymn of our nursery days, which bids us leave biting to the dogs, we see most plainly how firmly planted an animal root lies at the bottom of our proud humanity. Ages of civilisation have not succeeded in eradicating some of the most characteristic and unpleasant impulses of the brute.

At the same time a child's passionateness is more than a brute instinct. He suffers consciously; he realises himself in lonely antagonism to a world. This is seen in the bodily attitude of dejection which often follows the more vigorous stage of the fit, when the little Ishmaelite, growing aware of the impotence of his anger, is wont to throw himself on the floor and to hide his head in solitary wretchedness. This consciousness of absolute isolation and hostility reaches a higher phase when the opposing force is distinctly apprehended as human will. A dim recognition of the stronger will facing him brings the sense of injury, of tyrannous power.

Now this feeling of being injured and oppressed is human, and is fraught with moral possibilities. It is not as yet morally good; for the sense of injury is capable of developing, and may actually turn by-and-by into, hatred. Yet, as we shall see, it holds within itself a promise of something higher.

This predominance of self, this kinship with the unsocial brute, which shows itself in these germinal animosities, seems to be discoverable also in the unfeelingness of children. A common charge against them from those who are not on intimate terms with them, and sometimes, alas, from those who are, is that they are heartless and cruel.

That children often appear to the adult as unfeeling as a stone, is, I suppose, incontestable. The troubles which harass and oppress the mother may leave her small companion quite unconcerned. He either goes on playing with undisturbed cheerfulness, or he betrays a momentary curiosity about some trivial circumstance of her affliction which is worse than the absorption in play through its tantalising want of any genuine feeling. If, for example, she is ill, the event is interesting to him merely as supplying him with new treats. A little boy of four, after spending half an hour in his mother's sick-room, coolly informed his nurse: "I have had a very nice time, mamma's ill!" The order of the two statements is significant of the common attitude of mind of children towards others' sufferings.

When it comes to the bigger human troubles this want of fellow-feeling is still more noticeable. Nothing is more shocking to the adult observer of children than their coldness and stolidity in presence of death. While a whole house is stricken with grief at the loss of a beloved inmate the child is wont to preserve his serenity, being often taken with a shocking curiosity to peep into the dead room, and to get perhaps the gruesome pleasure of touching the dead body so as to know what "as cold as death" means, and at best showing only a feeling of awe before a great mystery.

No one, I think, will doubt that judged by our standards children are often profoundly and shockingly callous. But the question arises here, too, whether we are right in applying our grown-up standards. It is one thing to be indifferent with full knowledge of suffering, another to be indifferent in the sense in which a cat might be said to be so at the spectacle of your falling or burning your finger. We are apt to forget that a large part of the manifestation of human suffering is quite unintelligible to a little child.

Again, when an appeal to serious attention is

given, a child is apt to spy something besides the sadness. The little girl who wanted to touch, and to know the meaning of "cold as death," on going to see a dead schoolmate was not unnaturally taken up with the beauty of the scene, with the white hangings and the white flowers.

I am far from saying that the first acquaintance with death commonly leaves a child indifferent to the signs of woe. I believe, on the contrary, that children are frequently affected in a vague way by the surrounding gloom. In some cases, too, as published reminiscences of childhood show, the first acquaintance with the cruel monarch has sometimes shaken a child's whole being with an infinite, nameless sense of woe.

With this unfeelingness children are frequently charged with active unkindness, amounting to cruelty. La Fontaine spoke of the age of childhood as pitiless (*sans pitié*).

This appearance of cruelty will now and again show itself in dealings with other children. One of the trying situations of early life is to find oneself supplanted by the arrival of a new baby. Children, I have reason to think, are, in such circumstances, capable of coming shockingly near to a feeling of hatred. One little girl was taken with so violent an antipathy to a baby which she considered outrageously ugly as to make a beginning, fortunately only a feeble beginning, at smashing its head, much as she would no doubt have tried to destroy an ugly-looking doll.

Such malicious treatment of smaller infants is, I think, rare. More common is the exhibition of the signs of cruelty in the child's dealings with animals.

It is of this, indeed, that we mostly think when we speak of his cruelty.

At first nothing seems clearer than the evidence of malevolent intention in a child's treatment of animals. A little girl when only a year old would lift two kittens by the neck and try to stamp on them. Older children often have a way of treating even their pets with a similar roughness.

Yet I think we cannot safely say that such rough usage is intended to be painful. It seems rather to be the outcome of the mere energy of the childish impulse to hold, possess, and completely dominate his pet.

The case of destructive cruelty, as when a small boy crushes a fly, is somewhat different. Let me give a well-observed instance. A little boy of two years and two months, "after nearly killing a fly on the window-pane, seemed surprised and disturbed, looking round for an explanation, then gave it himself: ' Mr. Fly dom (gone) to by-by'. But he would not touch it or another fly again—a doubt evidently remained, and he continued uneasy about it." Here the arrest of life clearly brought a kind of shock, and we may safely say was not thought out beforehand. Children may pounce upon and maul small moving things for a number of reasons. The wish to gratify their sense of power—which is probably keener in children who so rarely gratify it than in grown-ups— will often explain these actions. To stop all that commotion, all that buzzing on the window-pane, by a single tap of the finger, that may bring a delicious thrill of power to a child. Curiosity, too, is a powerful incentive to this kind of maltreatment of animals.

Children have something of the anatomist's impulse to take living things apart, to see where the blood is, as one child put it, and so forth.

I think, then, that we may give the small offenders the benefit of the doubt, and not attribute their rough handling of animals to a wish to inflict pain, or even to an indifference to pain of which they are clearly aware. Wanton activity, the curiosity of the experimenter, and delight in showing one's power and producing an effect, seem sufficient to explain a large part of the unlearned brutality of the first years.

We have now looked at one of the darkest sides of the child and have found that though it is decidedly unpleasant it is not quite so ugly as it has been painted. Children are no doubt apt to be greedy, and otherwise unsociable, to be ferocious in their anger, and to be sadly wanting in consideration for others; yet it is some consolation to reflect that their savageness is not quite that of brutes, and that their selfishness and cruelty are a long way removed from a deliberate and calculating egoism.

The Promise of Humanity.

Pure Ishmaelite as he seems, however, a child has what we call the social instincts, and inconsistently enough no doubt he shows at times that after all he wants to join himself to those whom at other times he treats as foes. If he has his outbursts of temper he has also his fits of tenderness. If he is now dead to others' sufferings he is at another time taken with a most amiable childish concern for their happiness.

The germ of this instinct of attachment to society

may be said to disclose itself in a rude form in the
first weeks of life, when he begins to get used to and
to depend on the human presence, and is miserable
when this is taken from him.

In this instinct of companionship there is involved
a vague inarticulate kind of sympathy. Just as the
attached dog may be said to have in a dim fashion a
feeling of oneness with its master, so the child. The
intenser realisation of this oneness comes after separa-
tion. A girl of thirteen months was separated from her
mother during six weeks. On the return of the latter
she was speechless, and for some time could not bear
to leave her restored companion for a minute. A like
outbreak of tender sympathy is apt to follow a fit of
naughtiness when a child feels itself taken back to the
mother's heart.

Sympathy, it is commonly said, is a kind of imitation, and this is strikingly illustrated in its early
forms. A child has been observed under the age of
seven months to look unhappy, drawing down well
the corners of the mouth in the characteristic baby-
fashion when his nurse pretended to cry.

This imitative sympathy deepens with attachment.
We see something of it in the child's make-believe.
When, for example, a little girl on finding that her
mother's head ached pretended to have a bad head,
we appear to see the working of an impulse to get
near and share in others' experiences. The same
feeling shows itself in play, especially in the treatment of the doll, which has to go through all that
the child goes through, to be bathed, scolded, nursed
when poorly, and so forth.

From this imitative acting of another's trouble, so

as to share in it, there is but a step to that more direct apprehension of it which we call sympathy. Children sometimes begin to display such understanding of others' trouble early in the second year. One mite of fourteen months was quite concerned at the misery of an elder sister, crawling towards her and making comical endeavours by grunts and imitative movements of the fingers to allay her crying. I have a number of stories showing that for a period beginning early in the second year it is not uncommon for children to betray an exuberance of pity, being moved almost to tears, for example, when the mother says, "*Poor* uncle!" or when contemplating in a picture the tragic fate of Humpty Dumpty.

Very sweet and sacred to a mother are the first manifestations of tenderness towards herself. A child about the age of two has a way of looking at and touching its mother's face with something of the rapturous expression of a lover. Still sweeter, perhaps, are the first clear indications of loving concern. The temporary loss of her presence, due to illness or other cause, is often the occasion for the appearance of a deeper tenderness. A little boy of three spontaneously brought his story-book to his mother when she lay in bed ill; and the same child used to follow her about after her recovery with all the devotion of a little knight. At other times it is the suspicion of an injury to his beloved one, as when one little fellow seeing the strange doctor lay hold of his mother's wrist stood up like an outraged turkey-cock, backing into his mother's skirts, ready to charge the assaulter.

A deeper and thoughtful kind of sympathy often comes with the advent of the more reflective years.

9

Thought about the overhanging terror, death, is some-times its awakener. "Are you old, mother?" asked a boy of five. "Why?" she answered. "Because," he continued, "the older you are the nearer you are to dying." There was no doubt thought of his own loss in this question: yet there was, one may hope, a germ of solicitude for the mother too.

This first thought for others frequently takes the practical form of helpfulness. A child loves nothing better than to assist in little household occupations. A boy of two years and one month happened to overhear his nurse say to herself: "I wish that Anne would remember to fill the nursery boiler". "He listened, and presently trotted off; found the said Anne doing a distant grate, pulled her by the apron, saying: 'Nanna, Nanna!' (come to nurse). She followed, surprised and puzzled, the child pulling all the way, till, having got her into the nursery, he pointed to the boiler, and added: 'Go dare, go dare,' so that the girl comprehended and did as he bade her."

With this practical form of sympathy there goes a quite charming disposition to give pleasure in other ways. A little girl when just a year old was given to offering her toys, flowers, and other pretty things to everybody. Generosity is as truly an impulse of childhood as greediness, and it is odd to observe their alternate play. Early in the second year, too, children are wont to show themselves kindly by giving kisses and other pretty courtesies. In truth from about this date they are often quite charming in their ex-pressions of good will, so that the good Bishop Earle hardly exaggerates when he writes of the child: "He kisses and loves all, and when the smart of the rod is past, smiles on his beater ''. Later on a like amiable disposition will show itself in graceful turns of speech, as when a little girl, aged three and a quarter, petitioned her mother this wise : '' Please, mamma, will you pin this with the greatest pleasure ? ''

Just as there are these beginnings of affectionate concern for the mother and other people, so there is ample evidence of kindness to animals. The charge of cruelty in the case of little children is, indeed, seen to be a gross libel as soon as we consider their whole behaviour towards the animal world.

When once the first fear of the strangeness is mastered a child will generally take kindly to an animal. A little boy of fifteen months quickly overcame his fright at the barking of his grandfather's dog, and began to share his biscuits with him, to give him flowers to smell, and to throw stones for his amusement.

At a quite early age, too, children will show the germ of a truly humane feeling towards animals. The same little boy that bravely got over his fear of the dog's barking would, when nineteen months old, begin to cry on seeing a horse fall in the street. Stronger manifestations of pity are seen at a later age. A little boy of four was moved to passionate grief at the sight of a dead dog taken from a pond.

The indignation of children at the doings of the butcher, the hunter and others, shows how deeply pitiful consideration for animals is rooted in their hearts. This is one of the most striking manifestations of the better side of child-nature and deserves a chapter to itself.

The close absorbing sympathy which we often observe between a child and animals seems to come from a sense of common weaknesses and needs. Perhaps there is in it something of that instinctive impulse of helpless things to band together which we see in sheep and other gregarious animals. A mother once remarked to her boy, between five and six years old: "Why, R., I believe you are kinder to the animals than to me". "Perhaps I am," he replied, "you see they are not so well off as you are."

The same outpourings of affection are seen in the dealings of children with their toy babies and animals. Allowing for occasional outbreaks of temper and acts of violence, a child's intercourse with his doll or his toy "gee gee" is a wonderful display of loving solicitude; a solicitude which has something of the endurance of a maternal instinct.

Here, too, as we know, children vary greatly; there are the loving and the unloving moods, and there are the loving and the unloving children. Yet allowing for these facts, I think it may be said that in these first fresh outgoings of human tenderness we have a comforting set off to the unamiable manifestations described above.

The Lapse into Lying.

The other main charge against children is that they tell lies. According to many, children are in general accomplished little liars, to the manner born, and equally adept with the mendacious savage. Even writers on childhood who are by no means prejudiced against it lean to the view that lying is instinctive and universal among children.

Now it is surely permissible to doubt whether little children have so clear an apprehension of what we understand by truth and falsity as to be liars in this full sense. Much of what seems shocking to the adult unable to place himself at the level of childish intelligence and feeling will probably prove to be something far less serious.

To begin with those little ruses and dissimulations which are said to appear almost from the cradle in the case of certain children, it is plainly difficult to bring them into the category of full-fledged lies. When, for example, a child wishing to keep a thing hides it, and on your asking for it holds out empty hands, it would be hard to name this action a lie, even though there may be in it a germ of deception. These little ruses or "acted lies" seem at the worst to be attempts to put you off the scent in what is regarded as a private matter, and to have the minimum of intentional deception. This childish passion for guarding secrets may account for later and more serious-looking falsehoods.

There is a more alarming appearance of mendacity when the child comes to the use of language and proffers statements which, if he reflected, he might know to be false. Even here, however, we may easily apply grown-up standards unfairly. Anybody who has observed children's play and knows how real to them their fancies become for the moment will be chary of applying to their sayings the word "lie". There may be solemn sticklers for truth who would be shocked to hear the child when at play saying, "I am a coachman," "Dolly is crying," and so forth. But the discerning see nothing to be alarmed at here.

On the same level of moral obliquity I should be disposed to place those cases where a child will contradictingly say the opposite of what he is told. A little French boy was overheard saying to himself: "Papa parle mal, il a dit *sevette*, bébé parle bien, il dit *serviette*". Such reversals may be a kind of play too : the child not unnaturally gets tired now and then of being told that he is wrong, and for the moment imagines himself right and his elders wrong, immensely enjoying the idea.

The case looks graver when an "untruth" is uttered in answer to a question. A little boy on being asked by his mother who told him something, answered, "Dolly". "False, and knowingly false," somebody will say, especially when he learns that the depraved youngster instantly proceeded to laugh. But is not this laugh just the saving clause of the story, suggesting that it was play and the spirit of mischief at bottom ?

In this case, I suspect, there was co-operant a strongly marked childish characteristic, the love of producing an effect. A child has a large measure of that feeling which R. L. Stevenson attributes to the light-hearted Innes in *Weir of Hermiston*, "the mere pleasure of beholding interested faces". The well-known "cock and bull" stories of small children are inspired by this love of strong effect. It is the dramatic impulse of childhood endeavouring to bring life into the dulness of the serious hours. Childish vanity often assists, as where a little girl of five would go about scattering the most alarming kind of false news, as, for example, that baby was dead, simply to court attention and make herself of some importance.

A quick vivid fancy, a childish passion for acting a part, these, backed by a strong impulse to astonish, and a playful turn for contradiction and paradox, seem to me to account for most of this early fibbing and other similar varieties of early misstatement. Naughty it is, no doubt, in a measure ; but is it quite fairly branded as lying, that is, as a serious attempt to deceive?

In some cases, I think, the vivid play of imagination which prompts the untrue assertion may lead to a measure of self-deception. When, for example, an Italian child, of whom Signorina Lombroso tells us, who is out for a walk, and wanting to be carried says, "My leg hurts me and my foot too just here, I can't walk, I can't, I can't," it is possible at least that the vivid imagination of the South produces at the moment an illusory sense of fatigue. And if so we must hesitate to call the statement wholly a falsehood.

A fertile source of childish "untruth," which may be more true than untrue in the sense of expressing the conviction of the moment, is the wish to please. An emotional child who in a sudden fit of tenderness for his mother gushes out, "You're the best mother in the whole world!" may be hardly conscious of any exaggeration. There is more of artfulness in the flatteries which appear to involve a calculating intention to say the nice agreeable thing. Some children, especially little girls, are, I believe, adepts at these amenities. Those in whom the impulse is strong and dominant are perhaps those who in later years make the good society actors. Yet if there is a measure of untruth in such pretty flatteries, one needs to be superhuman in order to condemn them harshly.

The other side of this wish to please is the fear to give offence, and this, I suspect, may point to a more intentional and conscious kind of untruth. If, for example, a child is asked whether he does not like or admire something, his feeling that the questioner expects him to say "Yes" makes it very hard to say "No". Mrs. Burnett gives us a reminiscence of this early experience. When she was less than three, she writes, a lady visitor, a friend of her mother, having found out that the baby newly added to the family was called Edith, remarked to her: "That's a pretty name. My baby is Eleanor. Isn't that a pretty name?" On being thus questioned she felt in a dreadful difficulty, for she did not like the sound of "Eleanor," and yet feared to be rude and say so. She got out of it by saying she did not like the name as well as "Edith".

In such cases as this the fear to give offence may be reinforced by the mastering force of "suggestion". Just as the hypnotiser "suggests" to his subject the idea that he is ill, that the dirty water in this glass is wine, and so forth, compelling him to accept and act out the idea, so we all exercise a kind of suggestive sway over children's minds. Our leading questions, as when we say, "Isn't this pretty?" may for a moment set up a half belief that the thing must be so. Thus in a double fashion do our words control children's thoughts, driving them now into contradiction, drawing them at other times and in other moods into submissive assent. Wordsworth has illustrated how an unwise and importunate demand for a reason from a child may drive him into invention.[1]

I do not say that these are the only impulses which prompt to this early fibbing. From some records of the first years I learn that a child may drift into something like a lie under the pressure of fear, more especially fear of being scolded. One little fellow, more than once instanced in this work, a single child brought up wholly by his mother, perpetrated his first fib when he was about twenty-two months old. He went, it seems, and threw his doll down stairs in one of those capricious outbursts towards favourites which children share with certain sovereigns, then went to his mother and making great pretence of grief said, " Poor dolly tumbled ". If this had stood alone I should have been ready to look on it as a little childish comedy ; but the same child a month or two afterwards would invent a fib when he wanted his mother to do something. For example, he was one morning lying in bed with his mother and wanted much to get up. His mother told him to look for the watch and see what time it was. He felt under the pillow pretending to find and consult the time-teller, saying: " Time to get up ". Here it was clearly the force of the young will resisting an unpleasant check which excited the sober faculties to something like deception.

To say that our moral discipline with its injunctions, its corrections, is a great promoter of childish untruth may sound shocking, but it is I think an indisputable truth. We can see how this begins to work in the first years. For example, a mite of three

[1] See his poem, *Anecdote for Fathers, showing how the practice of lying may be taught.* (" Poems referring to the period of childhood.")

having in a moment of temper called her mother "monkey," and being questioned as to what she had said, replied: "I said *I* was a monkey". A child is often driven into such ruses by the instinct of self-protection.

Our system of discipline may develop untruth in other ways too. When, for example, punishment has been inflicted and its inflicter, relenting, asks: "Are you sorry?" or "Aren't you sorry?" the answer is exceedingly likely to be "No," even though this may at the moment be half felt to be untrue. From such partial untruths the way is easy to complete ones, as when a naughty little boy who is shut up in his room and kept without food, is asked: "Are you hungry?" and with the hardihood of a confirmed sinner answers "No," even though the low and dismal tone of the word shows how much the untruth goes against the grain.

I think there is no doubt, then, that at a certain age children may, more especially under a severe home authority, develop, apart from contagion, a tendency to falsehood. Some may see in this, as in childish fears and cruelties, rudiments of characteristics which belonged to remote uncivilised ancestors. However this be, it is hard to say that these fibs have that clear intention to deceive which constitutes a complete lie.

There are curious points in the manner of childish fibbing. A good many children seem to be like savages in distinguishing those to whom one is bound to speak the truth. The "bad form" of telling a lie to the head-master is a later illustration of the same thing. On the other hand it seems to be thought that there are people who are specially fitted to be the victims of untruth. Even young children soon find out who it is among the servants that being credulous supplies the best listener to their amazing inventions.

Another interesting point is the way in which the perfectly baseless fictions of children are apt to grow into permanent "stories". In the nursery and in the playground there are wont to be developed myths and legends which are solemnly believed by the simple-minded, and may be handed down to successors. In all such cases of propagated untruths the impulse of imitation and the tendency of the child's mind to accept statements uncritically are of course at work. The "lie" propagated by this influence of contagion very soon ceases to be a lie.

Fealty to Truth.

In order to understand what childish untruth really amounts to we must carefully note its after-effects on the perpetrator. It seems certain that many children experience a qualm of conscience when uttering that, of the falsity of which they are more or less aware. This is evidenced in the well-known devices by which the young casuist thinks to mitigate the lie; as when on saying what he knows to be false he adds mentally, "I do not mean it," "in my mind," or some similar palliative. Such subterfuges show a measure of sensibility, for a hardened liar would despise the shifts, and are curious as illustrations of the childish conscience and its unlearnt casuistry.

The remorse that sometimes follows lying, especially

the first lie, which catches the conscience at its ten-
derest, is much more than this passing qualm, and has
been remembered by many in later life.   Here is a
case.   A young lady whom I know remembers that
when a child of four she had to wear a shade over her
eyes.   One day on walking out with her mother she
was looking, child-wise, sidewards instead of in front,
and nearly struck a lamp-post.   Her mother then
scolded her, but presently remembering the eyes,
said : " Poor child, you could not see well ".   She
knew that this was not the reason, but she accepted
it, and for long afterwards was tormented with a sense
of having told a lie.

Such remorse, in certain cases prolonged beyond the
first lie, comes to the little offender as he or she lies in
bed and recalls the untruths of the day.   Some children
suffer greatly from this periodic reflection on their lies.

Some of the more poignant of the sufferings which
come to the sensitive child from saying what is false
are those of fear, fear of those terrific penalties which
religious teaching attaches to the lying tongue.   It
seems likely that childish devices for allaying their
qualms when saying what is untrue are intended
somehow to make things right with God, and so
to avoid the dreaded chastisement.   I am sure, too,
that the subsequent remorse, especially at night, is
very largely a dread of some awful manifestation of
God's wrath.

While I should set down much of this horror of
children at discovering themselves liars to a dread of
supernatural penalties, I should not set down the
whole.   I am disposed to think that there is another
force at work in the little people's consciousness.

In order to explain what I mean, I must begin by saying that a tendency towards conscious falsehood, though common, does not seem to be universal among children. Several mothers assure me that their children have never seriously put forth an untruth. I can say the same about two children who have been especially observed for the purpose.

I am ready to go further and to suggest that where a child is brought up normally, that is, in a habitually truth-speaking community, he tends, quite apart from moral instruction, to acquire a respect for truth. One may easily see that children accustomed to truth-speaking show all the signs of a moral shock when they are confronted with a false statement. I remember after more than twelve years one little boy's outbreaks of righteous indignation at meeting with untrue statements about his beloved horses and other things in one of his books, for which he had all a child's reverence. The idea of knowingly perpetrating an untruth, so far as I can judge, is simply awful to a child who has been thoroughly habituated to the practice of truthful statement. May it, then, not well be that when a preternatural pressure of circumstances pushes the child over the boundary line of truth, he feels a shock, a horror, a giddy and aching sense of having violated law—law not wholly imposed by the mother's command, but rooted in the very habits of social life?

Our inquiry has led us to recognise, in the case of cruelty and of lying alike, that children are by no means morally perfect, but have tendencies which, if not counteracted or held in check by others, will develop into the vices of cruelty and lying. On the other hand it has shown us that there are other and counteracting impulses, germs of human sympathy and of respect for the binding custom of truthfulness. So far from saying that child-nature is utterly bad or beautifully perfect, we should say that it is a disorderly jumble of impulses, each pushing itself upwards in lively contest with the others, some towards what is bad, others towards what is good. It is on this motley group of tendencies that the hand of the moral cultivator has to work, selecting, arranging, organising into a beautiful whole.

CHAPTER X.

REBEL AND SUBJECT.

CHILDREN are early confronted with our laws, and it is worth while asking how they behave in relation to these. Many persons seem to think that children generally are disobedient, lawless creatures; others, that some are obedient, others disobedient. Perhaps neither of these views is quite exact enough.

(a) The Struggle with Law : First Tussle with Authority.

Let us begin our study by looking a little more closely at what we call the disobedient attitude of children. That it exists nobody, surely, can well doubt. The very liveliness of young limbs and young wits brings their possessors into conflict with our sedate customs. The person who tries to wield authority over these small people is constantly introducing unpleasant checkings of vigorous impulse. A child has large requirements in the matter of movements and experiments with things, which are apt to clash with what the mother considers orderliness; when he is out of doors he exhibits a duck-like fondness for dirty water, whereas civilisation, represented by his tidy nurse, wills it that man should, at least when not in the arctic regions, be clean; he shows a perverse passion for fun and tricks when the mother thinks it the right time for serious talk, and so forth.   In these ways there comes the tussle with human law.

Yet surely, if we consider the matter impartially, we shall see that these collisions in the early years are perfectly normal and right.   In the interests of the race, at any rate, we ought perhaps to regard him as the better child, as the child of finer promise, who will not subject himself to human law without a considerable show of resistance.

The first and most impressive form of resistance to the laws of grown-ups is the use of physical force, which has already been touched on.   There is something pathetically comic in the spectacle of these mites resorting to the arbitrement of force, trying their small hand at pushing, striking, and the like ; and as we have seen the effort is wont soon to exhaust itself in childish despair.

As soon as our authority begins to assert itself in the issuing of commands the child's disposition to disobey, that is to have his way rather than ours, is apt to show itself now and again in decided refusals. When, let us say, the nurse gives up pulling him from the dirty pool, and bids him come away, he may very likely assert himself in an eloquent, " I won't," or less bluntly, " I can't come yet ".

Here, of course, there may be no wilful rejection of recognised law, but merely resistance to this particular disagreeable order coming from this particular person. Nevertheless we must, I fear, admit that such refusals to obey orders have in them something of true lawlessness.   The whole attitude of the child when he thus "tries on " defiance of commands is certainly suggestive of the rebel's temper. Nobody is so completely reckless as the child-rebel. When the fit is on him he pays not the least attention to the most awful of warnings. One little offender of four when he was reminded by his sister—two years older—that he would be shut out from heaven retorted impiously, "I don't care"; adding, for reasons best known to himself, "uncle won't go—I'll stay with him".

Evading the Law.

In addition to this first impressive form of opposition there are later ones which plainly show the spirit of antagonism. The conflict with law now takes on the aspect of evasion or "trying it on".

One of the simplest of these childish tricks is the invention of an excuse for not instantly obeying a command, as "Come here!" "Don't tease pussy!" A child soon finds out that to say "I won't" when he · is bidden to do something is indiscreet as well as vulgar. He wants to have his own way without resorting to a gross breach of good manners, so he replies insinuatingly, "I's very sorry, but I's too busy," or in some such conciliatory words. This field of invention offers a fine opportunity for the imaginative child. A small boy of three years and nine months on receiving from his nurse the familiar order, "Come here!" at once replied, "I can't, nurse, I's looking for a flea," and pretended to be much engrossed in the momentous business of hunting for this quarry in the blanket of his cot. The little trickster is such a lover of fun that he is pretty certain to betray his ruse in a case like this, and our small flea-catcher, we are told,

10

laughed mischievously as he proffered his excuse. Such sly fabrications may be just as naughty as the uninspired excuses of a stupidly sulky child, but it is hard to be quite as much put out by them.

It is a further refinement when the staunch little lover of liberty sets about "easing" the pressure of commands. If, for example, he is told to keep perfectly quiet because mother or father wants to sleep, he will prettily plead for the reservation of whispering ever so softly. If he is forbidden to ask for things at the table he will resort to sly indirect re-minders of what he wants, as when a boy of five and a half years whispered audibly: "I hope somebody will offer me some more soup," or when a girl of three and a half years, with more subtle insinuation, observed on seeing the elder folk eating cake : "I not asking".

A like astuteness will show itself in meeting the dismal accusations and scoldings. Sometimes the fault-finding is daringly ignored, and the small culprit, after keeping up an excellent appearance of listening, proceeds in the most artless way to talk about some-thing more agreeable, or, what is worse, to criticise the manner of his correction ; as when a small boy inter-rupted his mother's well-prepared homily by remark-ing : "Mamma, when you talk you don't move your upper jaw".

In cases in which no attempt is made to ignore the accusation, the small wits are wont to be busy dis-covering exculpations. Here we have the ruses, often crude enough, by which the little culprit tries to shake off moral responsibility, to deny the author-ship of the "naughty" action. The blame is put on anybody or anything—if there is no other scape-goat in view, then on the hands or other "bodily agents". This last device is sometimes hit upon very early, as when a mite of two who was told to stop crying gasped out : " Elsie cry—*not* Elsie cry—tears cry —naughty tears!" We find too at an early age a suggestion of fatalism, as when a boy of three who was blamed for not eating his crusts, and his pro- cedure contrasted with that of his virtuous sire, re- marked : "Yes, but, papa, you see God had made you and me different ".

Next to these denials of the "naughty" action come attempts at justification. Sometimes these look like pitiful examples of quibbling. A boy had been rough with his baby brother. His mother chid him, telling him he might hurt baby. He then asked his mother, " Isn't he my own brother?" and on his mother ad- mitting so incontestable a proposition, exclaimed triumphantly, "Well, you said I could do what I liked with *my own* things". At other times they have a dreadful look of being fibs invented for the purpose of covering a fault. Under a severe mode of discipline a child is apt, as already hinted, to slip over the boundary line of truth in his self-protective efforts to escape blame and punishment.

One other illustration of this keen childish dialectic when face to face with the accuser deserves to be touched on. The sharpened faculties have something of a lawyer's quickness in detecting a flaw in the in- dictment. Any exaggeration into which a feeling of indignation happens to betray the accuser is instantly pounced upon. If, for example, a child is scolded for pulling kitty's ears and making her cry it is enough for the little stickler for accuracy to be able to say:

"I wasn't pulling kitty's *ears*, I was only pulling *one* of her ears". The ability to deny the charge in its initial form gives him a great advantage, and robs the accusation in its amended form of much of its sting. Whence, by the way, one may infer that wisdom in managing children shows itself in nothing more than in a scrupulous exactness in the use of words.

The Plea for Liberty.

While there are these isolated attacks on various points of the daily discipline, we see now and again a bolder line of action in the shape of a general protest against its severity. Sometimes the parental authority is contrasted unfavourably with that of some other mother. The small boy who invented a family, *viz.*, a mother called Mrs. Cock and her little boys, frequently referred to this lady for the purpose of giving point to protests against the severity of the real mother. "For instance (writes the latter) when mother refuses her paint-box as a plaything, or declines to supply unlimited note-paper for 'scwibbleation,' a reproachful little voice is heard, 'Mrs. Cock always gives her paint-box and all her paper to my little boys'. A pause. Then follows suggestively: 'I fink she loves them vewy much'."[1] On the other hand, if the child accepts the mother's plea, that she has to impose restraints because she is a good mother, he is apt to wish that she were a shade less good. A boy of four had one morning to remain in bed till ten

[1] From a published article by Mrs. Robert Jardine (compare above, pp. 16, 17).

o'clock as a punishment for misbehaviour. He proceeded to address his mother in this wise: "If I had any little children I'd be a worse mother than you—I'd be quite a bad mother; I'd let the children get up directly I had done my breakfast at any rate".

Enough has been said to illustrate the ways in which the natural child kicks against the imposition of restraints on his free activity. He begins by showing himself an open foe to authority. For a long time after, while making a certain show of submission, he harbours in his breast something of the rebel's spirit. He does his best to evade the most galling parts of the daily discipline, and displays an admirable ingenuity in devising excuses for apparent acts of insubordination. And, lastly, where candour is permitted, he is apt to prove himself an exceedingly acute critic of the system which is imposed on him.

All this, moreover, seems to show that a child objects not only to the particular administration under which he happens to live, but to all law as implying restraints on free activity. Thus, from the child's point of view, so far as we have yet examined it, punishment as such is a thing which ought not to be.

So strong and deep-reaching is this antagonism to law and its restraints apt to be that the common longing to be "big" is, I believe, largely grounded on the expectation of liberty. To be big seems to the child more than anything else to be able to do what one likes without interference from others. "Do you know," asked a little fellow of four years, "what I shall do when I'm a big man? I'll go to a shop and buy a bun and pick out all the currants." One must have left in him much of the child in order to understand the fascination of that forbidden pleasure of daintily selecting the currants.

(b) *On the Side of Law.*

If, however, we look closer we shall find that this hostility is not the whole, perhaps not the most fundamental part, of a child's attitude towards law. It is evident that the early criticism of parental government referred to above, so far from implying rejection of all rule, plainly implies its acceptance. Some of the earliest and bitterest protests against interference are directed against what looks to the child irregular or opposed to law, as when, for example, he is allowed for some time to use a pair of scissors as a plaything, and is then suddenly deprived of it. And does not all the exercise of childish ingenuity in excuses imply in an indirect way that *if he had done* what is described in the indictment it would be naughty and deserving of punishment?

Other facts in early life bear out the conjecture that a child has law-abiding as well as law-resisting impulses. I think we may often discern evidence of this in his suffering when in disgrace. When he is too young perhaps to feel the shame, he will feel, and acutely too, the estrangement, the loneliness, the sudden shrinkage of his beloved world. The greater the love and the dependence, the greater will be this feeling of devastation. The same little boy who said to his mother: "I'd be a worse mother," emarked to her a few months later that if he could say what he liked to God it would be: "Love me when I'm naughty".

There is, perhaps, in this childish suffering often something more than the sense of being homeless and outcast. A child of four or five may, I conceive, when suffering disgrace have a dim consciousness of having broken with his normal orderly self, of having set at defiance that which he customarily honours and obeys.

Now this setting up of an orderly law-abiding self seems to me to imply that there are impulses which make for order. A child, as I understand the little sphinx, is at once the subject of ever-changing caprices —whence the delight in playful defiance of all rule and order—and the reverer of custom, precedent, rule. And, as I conceive, this reverence for precedent and rule is the deeper and the stronger impulse.

The Young Stickler for the Proprieties.

I believe that those who know young children will agree with me that they show an instinctive respect for what is customary and according to rule, such as a particular way of taking food, dressing, and definite times for doing this and that. Nor can we regard this as merely a reflection of our respect for law, for as we shall presently see it reaches far beyond the limits of the rules laid down by adults. It seems to be a true instinct which comes before education and makes education possible. It is related to habit, the great principle which runs through the whole of life.

The first crude manifestation of this disposition to make rule is seen in the insistence on the customary, as to the places of things, the order of procedure at meals and such like. The little boy of two, often quoted here, showed a punctilious feeling for order in the placing of things. He protested one morning in his mother's bedroom against a hair-brush being placed on the washing-stand near the tooth-brushes, saying quaintly: "That toof-brush is a brush one". Older children are apt to be sticklers for order at the meal-table: thus, the cup and the spoon have to be put in precisely the right place. Similarly, the sequences of the day, *e.g.*, the lesson before the walk, the walk before bed, have to be rigorously observed. This feeling for order may develop itself even where the system of parental government is by no means characterised by rigorous insistence on such minutiæ of procedure.

This impulse to extend rule appears more plainly in many of the little ceremonial observances of the child. Very charmingly is this respect for rule exhibited in all dealings with animals, also dolls and other pets. Not only are they required to do things in a proper orderly manner, but people have to treat them with due deference. One little fellow when saying good-night to his mother insisted on her going through with his doll precisely the same round of kissing and hand-shaking that he required in his own case.

This jealous regard for ceremony and the proprieties of behaviour is seen in the enforcement of rules of politeness by children who will extend them far beyond the scope intended by the parent. A delightful instance of this fell under my own observation, as I was walking on Hampstead Heath. It was a spring day, and the fat buds of the chestnuts were bursting into magnificent green plumes. Two well-dressed "misses," aged, I should say, about nine and eleven, were taking their correct morning walk. The elder called the attention of the younger to one of the trees, pointing to it. The younger exclaimed in a highly shocked tone : "Oh, Maud (or was it ' Mabel ' ?), you know you *shouldn't* point ! "

The domain of prayer well illustrates the same tendency. The child is wont, as we have seen, to think of God as a very, very grand person, and naturally, therefore, extends to him all the courtesies he knows of. Thus he must be addressed politely with the due forms, " Please," " If you please," and the like. The German child shrinks from using the familiar form " Du " in his prayers. As one maiden of seven well put it in reply to a question why she used " Sie " (the polite form of " you ") in her prayers : " Ich werde doch den lieben Gott nicht Du nennen : ich kenne ihn ja gar nicht " (But I mustn't call God "thou" : I don't know him, you see). On the other hand, God must not be kept waiting. "Oh, mamma," said a little boy of three years and eight months (the same that was so insistent about the kissing and hand-shaking), "how long you have kept me awake for you ; God has been wondering so whenever I was going to say my prayers." All the words must be nicely said to him. A little boy, aged four and three-quarter years, once stopped in the middle of a prayer and asked his mother : "Oh! how do you spell that word ? " The question is curious as suggesting that the child may have regarded his silent communication to the far-off King as a kind of letter.

The Enforcer of Rules.

Not only do children thus of themselves extend the

scope of our commands, they show a disposition to make rules for themselves. If, after being told to do a thing on a single occasion only, a child is found repeating the action on other occasions, this seems to show the germ of a law-making impulse. A little boy of two years and one month was once asked to give a lot of old toys to the children of the gardener. Some time after, on receiving some new toys, he put away, of his own accord, his old ones as before for the less fortunate children.

That the instinct for order assists moral discipline may be seen in the fact that children are apt to pay enormous deference to our rules. Nothing is more suggestive here than their talk among themselves, the emphasis they are wont to lay on the "must" and "must not". The truth is that children have a tremendous belief in the sacredness of rules.

This recognition of the absolute imperativeness of a rule properly laid down by the recognised authority is seen in the frequent insistence on its observance in new circumstances. It has been pointed out by Professor Preyer that a child of two years and eight months will follow out the prohibitions of the mother when he falls into other hands, sternly protesting, for example, against the nurse giving him the forbidden knife at table. Very proper children rather like to instruct their aunts and other ignorant persons as to the right way of dealing with them, and will rejoice in the opportunity of setting them straight even when it means a deprivation for themselves. The self-denying ordinance, "Mamma doesn't let me have many sweets," is by no means beyond the powers of a very correct little person.

A still clearer evidence of this respect for law as such, apart from its particular enforcement by the parent, is supplied by children's way of extending the rules imposed on themselves to others. No trait is better marked in the normal child than the impulse to subject others to his own disciplinary system. With what amusing severity are they wont to lay down the law to their dolls, and to their animal playmates, subjecting them to precisely the same prohibitions and punishments as those to which they themselves are subject! Nor do they stop here. They enforce the duties just as courageously on their human elders. A mite of eighteen months went up to her elder sister, who was crying, and with perfect mimicry of the nurse's corrective manner, said: "Hush! hush! papa!" pointing at the same time to the door.

This judicial bent of the child is a curious one and often develops a priggish fondness for setting others morally straight. Small boys have to endure much in this way from the hands of slightly older sisters proficient in matters of law and delighting to enforce the moralities. But sometimes the sisters lapse into naughtiness, and then the small boys have their chance. They too can on such occasions be priggish if not downright hypocritical. A little boy had been quarrelling with his sister named Muriel just before going to bed. On kneeling down to say his prayers and noticing that Muriel was sitting near and listening, he prayed aloud in this wise, "Please, God, make Muriel a good girl," then looked up and said in an angry voice, "Do you hear that, Muriel?" and after this digression resumed his petition.

This mania for correction shows itself too in rela-

tion to the authorities themselves. A collection of
rebukes and expositions of moral precept supplied by
children to their erring parents would be amusing
and suggestive. Here is an example : A boy of two
—the moral instruction of parents by the child begins
betimes—would not go to sleep when bidden to do so
by his father and mother. At length the father, losing
patience, addressed him with a man's fierce emphasis.
This mode of admonition so far from cowering the
child simply offended his sense of propriety, for he rejoined : " You s'ouldn't, s'ouldn't, Assum (*i.e.*, ' Arthur,'
the father's name), you s'ould speak nicely ".

We may now turn to what some will regard as still
clearer evidence of a law-fearing instinct in children,
viz., their spontaneous self-submission to its commands. We are apt to think of these little ones as
doing right only when under compulsion : but this is
far from the truth. A very young child will show
the germ of a disposition freely to adopt a law. A
little girl, when only twenty months old, would, when
left by her mother alone in a room, say to herself :
" Tay dar " (Stay there). About the same time, after
being naughty and squealing " like a railway-whistle,"
she would after each squeal say in a deep voice, " Be
dood, Babba " (her name). In like manner the little
boy often quoted at the age of twenty months said
to himself when walking down the garden, " Sonny
darling, mind nettles ". Here, no doubt, we see
quaint mimicries of the mother's fashion of control,
but they seem, too, to indicate a movement in the
direction of self-control.

Very instructive here is the way in which children
will voluntarily come and submit themselves to our

discipline. The girl just quoted, when less than two years old, would go to her mother and confess some piece of naughtiness and suggest the punishment. A little boy aged two years and four months was deprived of a pencil from Thursday to Sunday for scribbling on the wall-paper. His punishment was, however, tempered by permission to draw when taken downstairs. On Saturday he had finished a picture downstairs which pleased him. When his nurse fetched him she wanted to look at the drawing, but the boy strongly objected, saying : " No, Nanna (name for nurse), look at it till Sunday ". And sure enough when Sunday came, and the pencil was restored to him, he promptly showed nurse his picture.

That there is this tendency to fall in with punishment for breach of rule is borne out by some recent questionings of school children in America as to their views of the justice of their punishments. The results appear to show that they regard a large part of their corrections for naughtiness as a matter of course, the younger ones being apparently harsher in their views of what constitutes a proper punishment than the older ones.

These evidences of an impulse to look on correction as a quite proper thing are corroborated by stories of self-punishment. Here is an example : A girl of nine had been naughty, and was very sorry for her misbehaviour. Shortly after she came to her lesson limping, and remarked that she felt very uncomfortable. Being asked by her governess what was the matter with her she said : " It was very naughty of me to disobey you, so I put my right shoe on to my left foot and my left shoe on to my right foot ".

The facts here briefly illustrated seem to me to show that there is in the child from the first a rudiment of true law-abidingness, which exists side by side and struggles with the childish love of liberty and re-belliousness. And this is a force of the greatest consequence to the disciplinarian. It is something which takes side in the child's breast with the reasonable governor and the laws which he or she administers. It secures in many cases, at least, a ready compliance with a large part of the discipline enforced.

CHAPTER XI.

ONE of the most interesting phases of a child's activity is its groping after what we call art. Although a decided bent towards some special form of our art may be rare among children, most of them betray some rudiment of a feeling for beauty and of an impulse to produce it. It will be well to begin by glancing at the responses of children to the various presentations of beauty in nature and art, and then to examine their attempts at artistic production.

The Greeting of Beauty.

In looking in a young child for responses to the beauty of things, we must not, of course, expect a clear appreciation of its several phases. Here our aim will be to collect evidences of a natural feeling which may afterwards under favourable conditions grow into a discerning taste.

Even in infancy we may detect in the movements of the arms, the admiring cooing sounds, this greeting of nature's beauty as of something kindred. In the home interior it is commonly some bit of bright light, especially when it is in movement, which first charms the eye of the novice ; the dancing fire-flame, for example, the play of the sunlight on a bit of glass or a gilded frame, the great globe of the lamp just created. In some cases it is a patch of bright colour or a gay pattern on the mother's dress which calls forth a full vocal welcome in the shape of baby "talking". In the out-of-door scene, too, it is the glitter of the running water, or a meadow all white with daisies, which captivates the glance. Light, the symbol of life's joy, seems to be the first language in which the spirit of beauty speaks to a child.

A feeling for the charm of colour comes distinctly later. The first pleasure from coloured toys and pictures is hardly distinguishable from the welcome of the glad light, the delight in mere brightness. This applies pretty manifestly to the strongly illumined rose-red curtain which Professor Preyer's boy greeted with signs of satisfaction at the age of twenty-three days. Later on, too, when it is possible to test a child's feeling for colour, it has been found that a decided preference is shown for the bright or "luminous" tints, viz., red and yellow. An American observer, Miss Shinn, tells us that her niece in her twenty-eighth month had a special fondness for the daffodils—the bright tints of which allured, as we know, an older maiden, and, alas! to the place whence all brightness was banished. Among the other coloured objects which captivated the eye of this little girl were a patch of white cherry blossom, and a red sun-set sky. Such observations might easily be multiplied. Whiteness, it is to be noted, comes, as we might expect, with the brighter tones of the other colours among the first favourites.

At what age a child begins to appreciate the value of colour as colour, to like blue or red for its own sake and apart from its brightness, it is hard to say. The experiments made so far are not conclusive, though they seem to show that taste for colour does not always develop along the same lines.   Thus, according to the observer of one child, blue is one of the first to be preferred, though this is said not to be true of other children.   Later on, I believe, a child is wont to have his favourite colour, and to be ready to defend it against the preferences of others.

Liking for a single colour is a considerably smaller display of mind than an appreciation of the relation of two colours.   Many adults, it is said, hardly have a rudiment of this feeling, pairing the most fiercely antagonistic tints.   Common observation shows that most children, like the less cultivated adults, prefer juxtapositions of colours which are strongly opposed, such as blue and red or blue and yellow.   It would be interesting to know whether there is any general preference as between these two combinations.   It is, of course, a long step from this recognition of the contrast and mutual emphasising of colour to that of its quiet harmonious combinations.

That little children have their likings in the matter of form is, I think, indisputable, but they are not those of the cultivated adult.   One of the first out-goings of admiration towards form is the child's praise of "tiny" things.   The common liking of children for small natural forms, *e.g.*, those of the lesser birds, insects, and sea-shells, is well known.   How they love to "pile up" the endearing epithets "wee," "tiny" (or "teeny"), and the rest!   Here, as in so many of these childish admirations, we have to do not with a purely æsthetic perception.   The feeling for the

11

tiny things probably has in it the warmth of a young personal sympathy.

If now we turn to the higher aspects of form, such as symmetry and proportion, we encounter a difficulty. A child may acquire while quite young and before any methodical education commences a certain feeling for regular form. But can we be sure that this is the result of his own observations? We have to remember that his daily life, where the home is orderly, helps to impress on him regularity of form. In the laying of the cloth on the dinner-table, for example, he sees the regular division of space enforced as a law. Every time he is dressed, or sees his mother dress, he has an object-lesson in symmetrical arrangement. And so these features take on a kind of moral rightness before they are judged of as pleasing to the eye and as beautiful. The feeling for proportion, as, for example, between the height of a horse and that of a house, is, as children's drawings show us, in general very defective

A susceptibility to the pleasures of light, colour, and certain simple aspects of form, may be said to supply the basis of a crude perception of beauty. A quite small child is capable of acquiring a real admiration for a beautiful lady, in the appreciation of which brightness, colour, grace of movement, the splendour of dress, all have their part, while the charm for the eye is often reinforced by a sweet and winsome quality of voice. Such an admiration is not of course a pure appreciation of beauty: awe, some feeling for the social dignity of dress, perhaps a longing to be embraced by the charmer, may all enter into it; yet delight in the *look* of a thing for its own sake is surely the core of the feeling.

Perhaps the nearest approach to a pure æsthetic enjoyment in these early days is the love of flowers. The wee round wonders with their mystery of velvety colour are well fitted to take captive the young eye. I believe most children who live among flowers and have access to them acquire something of this sentiment, a sentiment in which admiration for beautiful things combines with a kind of dumb childish sympathy. No doubt there are marked differences among children here. There are some who care only, or mainly, for their scent, and the keen sensibilities of the olfactory organ appear to have a good deal to do with early preferences and prejudices in the matter of flowers. Others again care for them mainly as a means of personal adornment, though I am disposed to think that this partially interested fondness is less common with children than with many adults.

In much of this first crude utterance of the æsthetic sense of the child we have points of contact with the manifestations of taste among uncivilised races. Admiration for brilliant colours, for moving things, such as feathers, is common to the two. Yet a child coming under the humanising influences of culture soon gets far away from the level of the savage. Perhaps his almost perfectly spontaneous love of tiny flowers is already a considerable advance on his so-called prototype.

Many adults assume that a child can look at a landscape as they look at it, taking in the whole picturesque effect. When he is taken to Switzerland and shown a fine "view," his eye, so far from seizing the whole, will provokingly pounce on some unimportant detail of the scene and give undivided attention to this,

That the eye of a child of ten or less can enjoy the reddening of a snow-peak, or the emergence of a bright green alp from the mountain mist, I fully believe. But it is quite another thing to expect him to appreciate great extent of view and all the unnameable relations of form, of light and shade, and of colour, which compose a landscape.

First Peep into the Art-world.

While Nature is thus speaking to a child through her light, her colour and her various forms, human art makes appeal also. In a cultured home a child finds himself at the precincts of the art-temple, and feels there are wondrous delights within if he can only get there.

One of the earliest of these appeals is to the ear. A child outside the temple of art hears its music before he sees its veiled beauties. I have had occasion to show how sadly new sounds may perturb the spirit of an infant. Yet these same waves of sound, which break upon and shake the young nerves, give them, too, their most delightful thrill. Nowhere in adult experience do pleasure and sadness lie so near one another as in music, and a child's contrasting responses, as he now shrinks away with trouble in his eyes, now gratefully reaches forth and falls into joyous sympathetic movement, are a striking illustration of this proximity.

In the case of many happy children·the interest in the sounds of things, *e.g.*, the gurgle of running water, the soughing of the trees, is a large one. An approach to æsthetic pleasure is seen in the responses to rhythmic series of sounds.   Rhythm, it has been well said, is a universal law of life : all the activities of the organism have their regular changes, their periodic rise and fall.   The rhythm of a simple tune plays favourably on a child's ear, enhancing life according to this great law.   His ear, his brain, his muscles take on a new joyous activity, and the tide of life rises higher.   Nursery rhymes, which, it has recently been suggested, should be banished, bring something of this joy of ordered movement, and help to form the rhythmic ear.

With this feeling for rhythm there soon appears a discerning feeling for quality of tone.   First of all, I suspect, comes the appreciation of moderation and smoothness of sound ; it is the violent sounds which mostly offend the young ear.   A child's preference for the mother's singing is, perhaps, a half reminiscence of the soft-low tones of the lullaby. Purity or sweetness of tone, little by little, makes itself felt, and a child takes dislikes to certain voices as wanting in this agreeable quality.   Much later, in the case of all but gifted children, do the mysteries of harmony begin to take on definite form and meaning.

The arts which give to the eye semblances or representations of objects appeal to a child much more through his knowledge of things.   The enjoyment of a picture means the understanding of it as a picture, and this requires a process of self-education.   A child begins to make acquaintance with the images of things when set before a mirror.   Here he can inspect what he sees, say the reflection of the face of his mother or nurse, and compare it at once with the original.

With pictures there is no such opportunity of

directly comparing with the original, and children have to find out as best they may what the drawings in their picture-books mean.

A dim discernment of what a drawing represents may appear early. A little boy was observed to talk to pictures at the end of the eighth month. A girl of forty-two weeks showed the same excitement at the sight of a life-size painting of a cat as at that of a real cat. Another child, a boy, recognised pictures of animals by spontaneously naming them "bow-wow," etc., at the age of ten months.

The early recognition of pictured objects, of which certain animals have a measure, is often strikingly discerning. A child a little more than a year old has been known to pick out her father's face in a group of nine, the face being scarcely more than a quarter of an inch in diameter.

Another curious point in this early deciphering of drawings and photographs is that a child seems indifferent to the *position* of the picture, holding it as readily inverted as in its proper position. One little girl of three and a half "does not mind (writes her father) whether she looks at a picture the right way up or the wrong; she points out what you ask for, eyes, feet, hands, tail, etc., about equally well whichever way up the picture is, and never asks to have it put right that she may see it better". A like indifference to the position of a picture, and of a letter, has been observed among backward races.

Surprising as this early recognition of pictures undoubtedly is, it is a question whether it necessarily implies any idea of the true nature of them, as being merely semblances or representations of things.

That children do not, at first, clearly seize the meaning of pictures is seen in the familiar fact that they will touch them just as they touch shadows, and otherwise treat them as if they were tangible realities. One little girl attempted to smell at the trees in a drawing and pretended to feed some pictorial dogs. This may have been half play. But here is a more convincing example. A girl was moved to pity by a picture of a lamb caught in a thicket, and tried to lift the branch that lay across the animal. With less intelligent children traces of this tendency to take pictorial representation for reality may appear as late as four. One American boy having looked at a picture of people going to church in the snow, and finding on the next day that the figures in the drawing were exactly in the same position, seemed perplexed, and remarked naïvely: "Why, Mrs. C., these people haven't got there yet, have they?"

It is not surprising after this to learn that some children are slow in seizing the representative character of acting. If, for example, a father at Christmas-tide disguises himself as Santa Claus, his child will only too readily take him to be what he represents himself to be, and this when the disguise, especially in the matter of the voice, leaves much to be desired. Children, like uneducated adults, have been known to take a spectacle on the stage of a theatre too seriously. Yet their own play, which, though serious at the moment, is known afterwards to be "pretending," probably renders many of them particularly quick in interpreting dramatic play.

This tendency to take art-representations for realities reappears even in the mental attitude of a child towards his stories. A verbal narrative has of course in itself nothing similar to the scenes and events of which it tells. In this it differs from the semblance of the picture and of the dramatic spectacle. Yet a story, just because it uses our common forms of language and takes the guise of a narrative about people who lived at such a time and place, may well appear to a child's mind to tell of real events. At any rate we know that he is wont to believe tenaciously in the truth of his stories.

Careful observations of these first movements of the child's mind towards art will illustrate the variable directions of his taste. The preferences of a boy of four in the matter of picture-books tell us where his special interests lie, what things he finds pretty, and may supply a hint as to how much of a genuine æsthetic faculty he is likely to develop later on.

It is curious to note children's first manifestations of a sense of the pathetic and the comic as represented in art. Here marked differences present themselves. Those of a more serious turn are apt to show a curious preference for the graver aspects of things. They like stories, for example, with a certain amount of tension and even of thrill in them. There are others who disclose a special susceptibility to the more simple effects of pathos. There are sentimental children, as there are sentimental adults, who seem never happier than when the tears are ready to start. It may be suspected from the number of descriptions of early deaths in literature for the young that some at least must take pleasure in this kind of description. A child's strong feeling of attachment to animals is apt at a certain age to give to stories about the hardships of horses and the like something of an overpowering sadness.

The sense of the comic in children is a curious subject to which justice has not yet been done. The tendency to judge them by our grown-up standards shows itself in an expectation that their laughter will follow the directions of our own. Their fun is, I suspect, of a very elemental character. They are apt to be tickled by the spectacle of some upsetting of the proprieties, some confusion of the established distinctions of rank. Dress, as we have seen, has an enormous symbolic value for their mind, and any incongruity here is apt to be specially laughter-provoking. One child between three and four was convulsed at the sight of his baby bib fastened round the neck of his bearded sire. There is, too, a considerable element of rowdiness in children's sense of the comical, as may be seen by the enduring popularity of the spectacle of Punch's successful misdemeanours and bravings of the legal authority. The sense of humour which is finely percipient and half reflective is far from their level, as indeed it is from that of the average adult. Hence the fact familiar to parents that stories which treat of child-life with the finer kind of humour may utterly fail to tickle a young reader.

First Ventures in Creation.

It is sometimes said that children are artists in embryo, that in their play and throughout their activity they manifest the germs of the art-impulse. It seems worth while to examine the saying.

There is no doubt that in much of the first spontaneous activity there is a trace of æsthetic feeling and the impulse to produce something pretty. Yet the feeling is in most children weak and vacillating, and is wont to be mixed with other and less noble ones.

One of the lower and mixed forms of artistic activity, in the case of the child and of the race alike, is personal adornment. The impulse to study appearances appears to reach far down in animal life. Two impulses seem to be at work here: to frighten or overawe others, as seen in the raising of feathers and hair so as to increase size, and to attract, which possibly underlies the habit of trimming feathers and fur among birds and quadrupeds. The same two impulses are said to lie at the root of the elaborate art of personal adornment developed by savages.

In the case of children brought up in the ways of civilisation where personal cleanliness and adornment are peremptorily enforced in the face of many a tearful protest, it seems at first vain to look for the play of instinctive tendencies. Yet I think if we observe closely we shall detect traces of a spontaneous impulse towards self-adornment. Children, like uncultured adults, are wont to prize a bit of finery in the shape of a string of beads or of daisies for the neck, a feather for the hat, and so forth. Imitation of the ways of their elders doubtless plays a part here, but it is aided by an instinct for adornment. Little girls perhaps represent the attractive function of adornment: they like to be thought pretty. Little boys when decking themselves out with tall hat and monstrously big clothes seem to be trying to put on an alarming aspect.

Since children are left so little free to deck themselves, it is of course hard to study the development
of æsthetic taste in this domain of their activity. Yet
their quaint attempts to improve their appearance
throw an interesting side-light on their æsthetic
preferences. While in general they have in their
hearts almost as much love of glitter, of gaudy colour,
as uncivilised adults, they betray striking differences of feeling ; some developing, for example, a
bent towards modest neatness and refinement, and
this, it may be, in direct opposition to the whole
trend of home influence.

Another domain of childish activity which is akin
to art is the manifestation of grace. A good deal
of the charm of movement, of gesture, of intonation,
in a young child may be unconscious, and as much a
result of happy physical conditions as the pretty
gambols of a kitten. Yet one may commonly detect
in graceful children the rudiment of an æsthetic feeling for what is nice, and also of the instinct to please.
There is, indeed, in these first actions, such as the kissing of the hand to other children in the street, something
of the simple grace and dignity of the more amiable
of those uncivilised races which we dishonour by
calling them savages. This feeling for pleasing
effect in bodily carriage and movement, in the use of
speech and gesture, is no doubt far from being a pure
art-activity. Traces of self-consciousness, of vanity,
are often discernible in it ; yet at least it attests the
existence of a certain appreciation of what is beautiful, and of something akin to the creative impulse of
the artist.

A true art-impulse is characterised by a pure love

of doing something which, either in itself as an action or in the material result which it produces, is beautiful. Into this there enters, at the moment at least, no consciousness of self. Now there is one field of children's activity which, as was suggested in an earlier chapter, is marked by just this absorption of thought in action for its own sake, and that is play.

To say that play is art-like has almost become a commonplace. Like art it is inspired and sustained by a pure love of producing. Like art, too, on its representative side, play aims at producing an imitation or semblance of something. The semblance may be plastic, residing in the material product of the action, as in making things such as castles out of cardboard or sand ; or it may be dramatic and reside in the action itself, as in much of the childish play already described.

The imitative impulse prompting to the production of the semblance of something appears very early in child-life. A good deal of the imitation wh'ch occurs in the second half year is the taking on, under the lead of another's example, of actions which are more or less useful. This applies, for example, to such actions as waving the hand in sign of farewell, and of course to vocal imitation of others' verbal sounds. At an early date we find, further, a perfectly useless kind of imitation which is more akin to that of art. A quite young child will, for example, *pretend* to do something, as to take an empty cup and carry out the semblance of drinking. The imitation of the sounds and movements of animals, which comes early too, may be said to be imitative in the more artistic sense, inasmuch as it has no aim beyond that of mimetic representation.

Later on, towards the third year, this simple type of imitative action grows more complex, so that a prolonged make-believe action may be carried out. A child, for example, occupies himself with pretending to be an organ-grinder's monkey, going duly and in order through the action of jumping down from his seat, and taking off his cap by way of begging for the stranger's contribution. Here, it is evident, we get something closely analogous to histrionic performance. This play-like performance, again, gradually divides itself into a more serious kind of action, analogous to serious drama, and into a lighter representaation of some funny scene, which has in it something akin to comedy.

Meanwhile, another form of imitation is developing, the fashioning of lasting semblances. Early illustrations of this impulse are the making of a river out of the gravy in the plate, the pinching of pellets of bread till they take on something of resemblance to known forms. One child, three years old, would occupy himself at table by turning his plate into a clock, in which the knife and fork were made to act as hands, and cherry stones put round the plate to represent the hours. Such table-pastimes are known to all observers of children, and have been prettily touched on by R. L. Stevenson in his essay on "Child's Play".

These formative touches are, at first, rough enough, the transformation being effected, as we have seen, much more by the alchemy of the child's imagination than by the cunning of his hands. Yet, crude as it is, and showing at first almost as much of chance as of design, it is a manifestation of the same plastic impulse which possesses the sculptor and the painter.

The more elaborate constructive play which follows—the building with cards and wooden bricks, the moulding with sand and clay, and the first spontaneous drawings—is the direct descendant of this rude formative activity. The kindergarten is, indeed, a kind of smaller art-world where the dramatic and plastic impulses of the child are led into orderly action.

In this imitative play we see from the first the artistic tendency to set forth what is characteristic in the things represented. Thus in the unstudied acting of the nursery, the nurse, the coachman, and the rest, are presented by a few broad touches; characteristic actions, such as pouring out the medicine, jerking the reins, being aided by one or two rough accessories, as the medicine bottle or the whip. In this way child's play, like primitive art, shows a certain unconscious selectiveness. It presents what is constant and typical, imperfectly enough no doubt. The same selection of broadly distinctive traits is seen where some individual person, *e.g.*, a particular newsboy or gardener, seems to be represented. A similar tendency to a somewhat bald typicalness of outline is seen in the first rude attempts of children to construct, whether with materials like cards or bricks, or with pencil, the semblance of a house, a garden and so forth.

As observation widens and grows finer, the first bald representation becomes fuller and more life-like. A larger number of distinctive traits is taken up into the play. Thus the coachman's talk becomes richer, fuller of reminiscences of the stable, etc., and so colour is given to the dramatic picture. Similarly with the products of the plastic impulse.

With this more realistic tendency to exhibit the

characteristic with something like concrete fulness we see the germ at least of the idealistic impulse to transcend the level of common things, to give prominence to what has value, to touch the representation with the magic light of beauty.   Even a small child playing with its coloured petals or its shells will show a rudiment of this artistic feeling for beautiful arrangement.

No doubt there are striking variations among children in this respect.   Play discloses in many ways differences of feeling and ideas : among others, in the unequal degrees of tastefulness of the play scene.   Yet the presence of an impulse, however rudimentary, to produce what has beauty and charm for the eye is a fact which we must recognise.

Along with this feeling for the sensuous effect of beauty we can discern the beginnings of fancy and invention whereby the idea represented is made more prominent and potent.   This tendency, like the others, shows itself in a crude form at first, as in the earlier and coarser art of the race.   In children's play we can see much of the uncultured man's love of strong effect. The pathos of the death of the pet animal or of the child has to be made obvious and strongly effective by a mass of painful detail ; the comic incident must be made broadly farcical by heavy touches of caricature ; the excitement of perilous adventure has to be intensified by multiplying the menacing forces and the thrilling situations.   Yet crude as are these early attempts at strengthening the feebleness of the actual they are remotely akin to the idealising efforts of true art.

Nevertheless, children's play, though akin to it, is

not completely art. As pointed out above, the action in a child's play is not intended as a dramatic spectacle. The small player is too self-centred, if I may so say. The scenes he acts out, the semblances he shapes with his hands, are not produced, as art is produced, for its own worth's sake, but rather as providing a new world into which he may retire and enjoy privacy. A child in playing a part does not " play " in order to delight others. " I remember," writes R. L. Stevenson, " as though it were yesterday, the expansion of spirit, the dignity and self-reliance, that came with a pair of mustachios in burnt cork *even when there was none to see.*" The same is true when children play at being Indians or what not: they are not " acting " in the theatrical sense of the word.

While, then, one can say that there is something akin to art in the happy semi-conscious activity of the child at play, we must add that, for the development of the true impulse of the artist, a good deal more is needed. The play-impulse will only get specialised into the art-impulse when it is illumined by a growing participation in the social consciousness, and by a sense of beauty and the æsthetic worth of things; when, further, it begins to concentrate itself on one mode of imitative activity, as, for example, dramatic represen-tation or drawing.

I have chosen here to deal with the more spon-taneous manifestations of an art-like impulse in chil-dren, rather than to describe their first attempts at art as we understand it. Here—in the case of all but those endowed with a genuine artistic talent—we are apt to find too much of the adult's educative in-fluence, too little of what is spontaneous and original.

At the same time, some of this art-activity, more particularly the first weaving of stories, is characteristic
enough to deserve a special study. I have made a
small collection of early stories, and some of them are
interesting enough to be quoted. Here is a quaint
example of the first halting manner of a child of two
and a half years as invention tries to get away from
the sway of models: "Three little bears went out a
walk, and they found a stick, and they poked the fire
with it, and they poked the fire and then went a
walk". Soon, however, the young fancy is apt to
wax bolder, and then we get some fine invention. A
boy of five years and a quarter living at the sea-side
improvised as follows. He related "that one day he
went out on the sea in a lifeboat, when suddenly he
saw a big whale, and so he jumped down to catch it;
but it was so big that he climbed on it and rode on it
in the water, and all the little fishes laughed so ".

With this comic story may be compared a more
serious not to say tragic one from the lips of a girl one
month younger, which is characterised by an almost
equal fondness for the wonderful. " A man wanted
to go to heaven before he died. He said, 'I don't
want to die, and I must see heaven!' Jesus Christ
said he must be patient like other people. He then
got *so* angry, and screamed out as loud as he could,
and kicked up his heels as high as he could, and they
(the heels) went into the sky, and the sky fell down
and broke the earth all to pieces. He wanted Jesus
Christ to mend the earth again, but he wouldn't, so
this was a good punishment for him." This last,
which is the work of one now grown into womanhood
and no longer a story-teller, is interesting in many

12

ways. The wish to go to heaven without dying is, as I know, a motive derived from child-life. The manifestations of displeasure could, one supposes, only have been written by one who was herself experienced in the ways of childish "tantrums". The naïve conception of sky and earth, and lastly the moral issue of the story, are no less instructive.

These samples may serve to show that in the stories of by no means highly gifted children we come face to face with interesting traits of the young mind, and can study some of the characteristic tendencies of early and primitive art. Of the later efforts to imitate older art, as verse writing, the same cannot, I think, be said. Children's verses, so far as I have come across them, are poor and stilted, showing all the signs of the cramping effect of models and rules to which the young mind cannot easily accommodate itself, and wanting in true childish inspiration. No doubt, even in these choking circumstances, childish feeling may now and again peep out. The first prose compositions, letters before all if they may be counted art, give more scope for the expression of this feeling and the characteristic movements of young thought, and might well repay careful study.

There is one other department of children's art which clearly does deserve to be studied with some care—their drawing. And this for the very good reason that it is not wholly a product of our influence and education, but shows itself in its essential characteristics as a spontaneous self-taught activity which takes its rise, indeed, in the play-impulse. To this I propose to devote my next and last chapter.

CHAPTER XII

FIRST PENCILLINGS.

A CHILD'S first attempts at drawing are not art proper, but a kind of play. As he sits at the table and covers a sheet of paper with line-scribble he is wholly self-centred, "amusing himself," as we say, and caring nothing about the production of a thing of æsthetic value.

Yet even in this infantile scribbling we see a tendency towards art-production in the effort of the small draughtsman to make his lines indicative of something to another's eyes, as when he bids his mother look at the "man," "gee-gee," or what else he cheerfully imagines his scribble to delineate. Such early essays to represent objects by lines, though commonly crude enough and apt to shock the æsthetic sense of the matured artist by their unsightliness, are closely related to art, and deserve to be studied as a kind of preliminary stage of pictorial design.

In studying what is really a large subject it will be well for us to narrow the range of our inquiry by keeping to delineations of the human figure and of animals, especially the horse. These are the favourite topics of the child's pencil, and examples of them are easily obtainable.

As far as possible I have sought spontaneous

drawings of quite young children, *viz.*, from between two and three to about six. In a strict sense, of course, no child's drawing is absolutely spontaneous and independent of external stimulus and guidance. The first attempts to manage the pencil are commonly aided by the mother or other instructor, who, moreover, is wont to present a model drawing, and, what is even more important at this early stage, to supply model-movements of the arm and hand. In most cases, too, there is some slight amount of critical inspection, as when she asks, "Where is papa's nose?" "Where is doggie's tail?" In one case, however, I have succeeded in getting drawings of a little girl who was carefully left to develop her own ideas. Even in the instances where adult supervision is apt to interfere, we can, I think, by patient investigation distinguish traits which are genuinely childish.

A child's drawing begins with a free aimless swinging of the pencil to and fro, which movements produce a chaos of slightly curved lines. These movements are purely spontaneous, or, if imitative, are so only in the sense that they follow roughly the directions of another's pencil.

In this first line-scribble there is no serious intention to trace a particular form. What a child seems to do in this rough imitation of another's movements is to make a tangle of lines, more or less straight, varied by loops, which in a true spirit of play he makes believe to be the semblance of "mamma," "pussy," or what not, as in Fig. 1 (*a*) and (*b*). Possibly in not a few cases the interpretation first suggests itself after the scribble, the child's fancy discerning some faint resemblance in his formless tangle to a human head, a cat's tail, and so forth.

Fig. 1 (a).[1]

Fig. 1 (b).[1]

This habit of scribble may persist after a child attempts a linear description of the parts of an object. Thus a little girl in her fourth year when asked to draw a cat produced the two accompanying figures (Fig. 2 (a) and (b)).

Here it is evident we have a phase of childish draw-

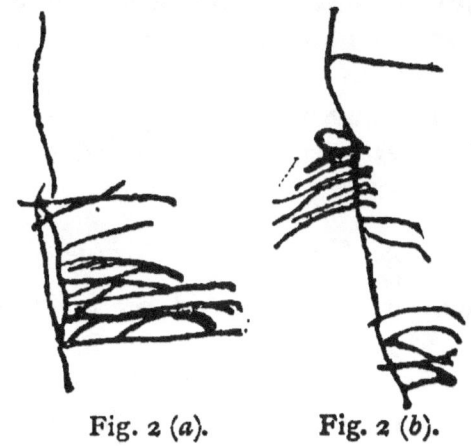

Fig. 2 (a).   Fig. 2 (b).

[1] Fig. 1 (a) is a drawing of a man by a child of twenty months, reproduced from Prof. M. Baldwin's *Mental Development*, p. 84; Fig. 1 (b) is a drawing of a man by a child of two years three months, reproduced from an article on children's drawings by Mr. H. T. Lukens in *The Pedagogical Seminary*, vol. iv. (1896).

ing which is closely analogous to the symbolism of language. The form of representation is chosen arbitrarily and not because of its likeness to what is represented. This element of symbolic indication will be found to run through the whole of childish drawing.

As soon as the hand acquires a certain readiness in drawing lines and closed lines or "outlines," and begins to connect the forms produced with the necessary movements, drawing takes on a more intentional character. The child now aims at constructing a particular linear representation, that of a man, a horse, or what not. These first attempts to copy in line the forms of familiar objects are among the most curious products of the child's mind. They follow standards and methods of their own; they are apt to get hardened into a fixed conventional manner which may reappear even in mature years. They exhibit with a certain range of individual difference a curious uniformity, and they have their parallels in what we know of the first crude designs of the untutored savage.

The Human Face Divine.

It has been wittily observed by an Italian writer, Signor Corrado Ricci, that children in their drawings reverse the order of natural creation by beginning instead of ending with man. It may be added that they start with the most dignified part of this crown of creation, *viz.*, the human head. A child's attempt to represent a man appears commonly to begin by drawing a sort of circle for the front view of the head. A dot or two, sometimes only one, sometimes as many as five, are thrown in as a rough way of indicating the features.

I speak here of the commoner form. There are however variations of this. Some children draw a squarish outline for head, but these are children *at school*. In one case, that of a little girl aged three years four months, the outline was not completed, the facial features being set between two vertical columns of scribble, which do duty for legs (Fig. 3). Sometimes the features are simply laid down without any

Fig. 3.[1]

enclosing contour ; and this arrangement appears not only in children's drawings but in those of savage adults.

The representation of the head some- times appears alone, but a strong ten- dency to bring in the support of the legs soon shows itself. This takes at first the crude device of a couple of vertical lines attached to the head (see Fig. 4).

Coming now to the mode of re- presenting the face, we find at an early stage the commencement of an attempt to differentiate the features. In drawings of children of three we frequently see that while the eyes are indicated by dots the nose is given as a

Fig. 4.

[1] Reproduced from the article already referred to, by Mr. Lukens.

short vertical line. Similarly when the mouth appears
it does so commonly as a horizontal line. We notice
that more attention is given to the problem of placing
a feature than to that of making a likeness of it.
Indeed this first drawing is largely a pointing out
or noting down of features without any serious effort
to draw them. The representation is a kind of local
description rather than a true drawing. Curious
differences appear in respect of the completeness of

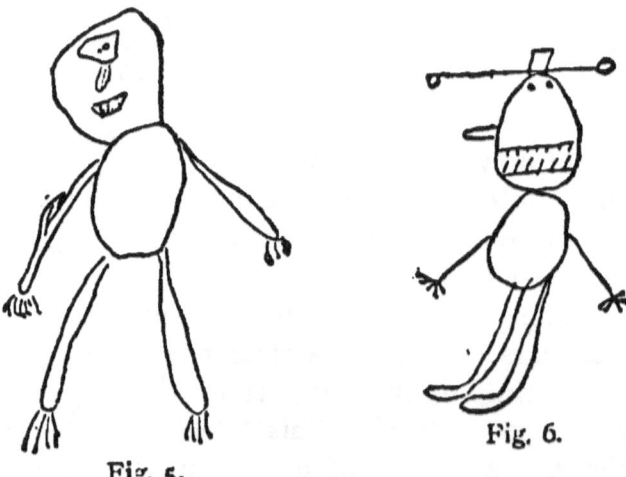

Fig. 5.

Fig. 6.

this linear noting or enumerating of features. The
nose more particularly appears and disappears in a
capricious way in the drawings of the same child.

Odd differences, reflecting differences of intelligence, show themselves in the management of this
diagram of the human face. One child, a Jamaica
girl of seven, went so far as to draw the face with
only one eye (Fig. 5). Again though, as I have said,
a child will try to give a correct local arrangement,

for example putting the nose between and below the eyes, he does not always reach accuracy of localisation. Many children habitually set the two eyes far up towards the crown of the head, as in Fig. 6. When the features begin to be represented by something more like a form we find in most cases a curious want of proportion. The eye, for instance, is often greatly exaggerated ; so is the mouth, which is sometimes drawn right across the face, as in Fig. 6.

As the drawing progresses we note a kind of evolution of the features. In the case of the eye, for example, we may often trace a gradual development, the dot being displaced by a small circle or ovoid, this last supplemented by a second outer circle, or by an arch or pair of arches. In like manner the mouth, from being a bare symbolic indication, gradually takes on form and likeness. There appears a rude attempt to picture the mouth cavity and to show those interesting accessories, the teeth. The nose, too, tries to look more like a nose by help of various ingenious expedients, as by drawing an angle, a triangle, and a kind of scissors arrangement in which the holders stand for the nostrils (see Fig. 7 (*a*) and (*b*) ; compare above, Fig. 4).

Ears, hair, and the other adjuncts come in later as after-thoughts. Much the same characteristics are observable in the treatment of these features.

The Vile Body.

At first, as I have observed, the trunk is commonly omitted. The indifference of the young mind to this is seen in the obstinate persistence of the first scheme of a head set on two legs, even when two arms are added and attached to the sides of the head. Indeed a child will sometimes complete the drawing by adding feet and hands before he troubles to bring in the trunk (see Fig. 8).

From this common way of spiking the head on two forked or upright legs there occurs an important deviation. The contour of the head may be left incomplete, and the upper part of the curve be run on into

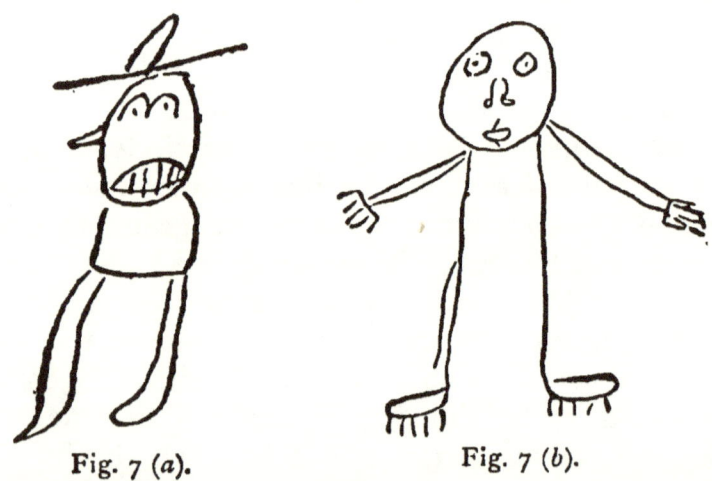

Fig. 7 (*a*).   Fig. 7 (*b*).

the leg-lines, as in the accompanying example by a Jamaica girl (Fig. 8).

The drawing of the trunk may commence in different ways. Sometimes a lame attempt is made to indicate it by leaving space between the head and the legs, that is, by not attaching the legs to the head. Another contrivance is where the space between the legs is shown to be the trunk by shading or by drawing a vertical row of buttons. In other cases the contour of the head appears to be elongated so as to serve for head and trunk. A better expedient is drawing a line across the two vertical lines and so marking off the trunk (see Fig. 9 (*a*) to (*d*)). In

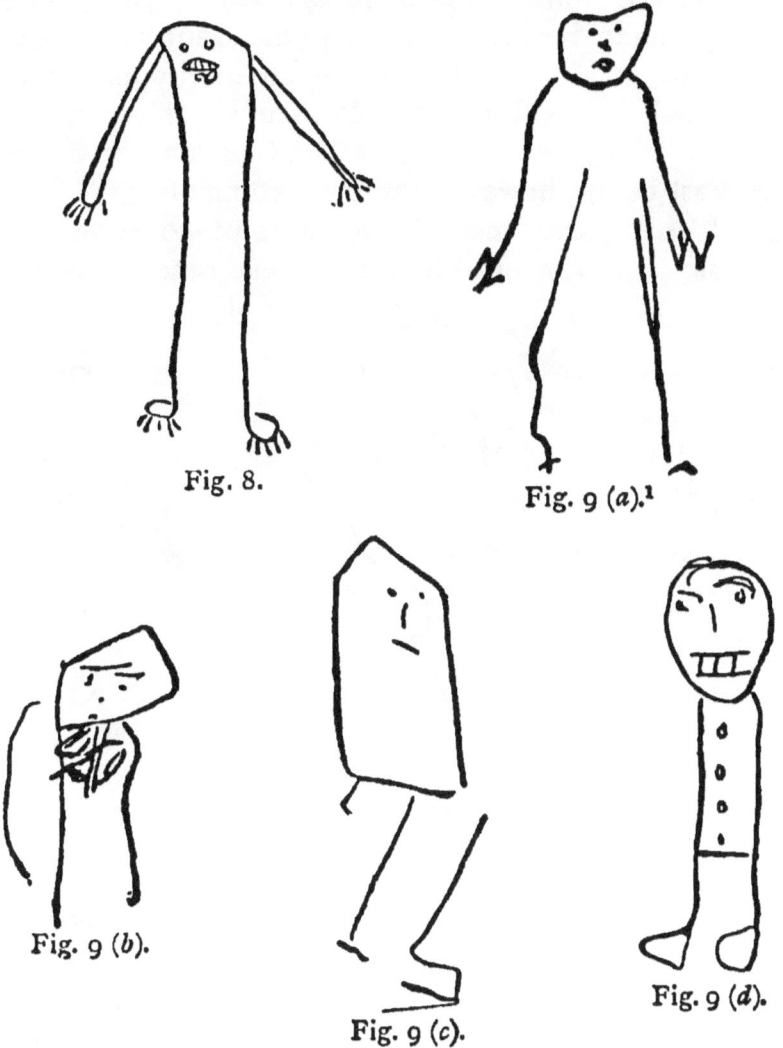

Fig. 8.

Fig. 9 (*a*).[1]

Fig. 9 (*b*).

Fig. 9 (*c*).

Fig. 9 (*d*).

[1] Fig. 9 (a) is a reproduction of a drawing of a girl of four and a half years, from Mr. Lukens' article.

drawings made by Brazilian Indians we see another device, *viz.*, a pinching in of the vertical lines (see Fig. 9 (e)).

After the trunk has been recognised by the young draughtsman he is apt to show his want of respect for it by making it absurdly small in proportion to the head, as in Fig. 10. It assumes a variety of shapes, triangular, rectangular, and circular or ovoid, this last being, however, the most common.

At this stage there is no attempt to show the joining on of the head to the trunk by means of the

Fig. 9 (e).

Fig. 10.

Fig. 11.

neck. When this is added it is apt to take the exaggerated look of caricature, as in Fig. 11.

A curious feature which not infrequently appears in this first drawing of the trunk is the doubling of the corporeal ovoid, one being laid upon the other. As this appears when a neck is added it looks like a clumsy attempt to indicate the pinch at the waist—presumably the female waist (see Fig. 12).

The introduction of the arms is very uncertain. To

the child, as also to the savage, the arms seem far less important than the legs, and are omitted in rather more than one case out of two. After all, the divine portion, the head, can be supported very well without their help.

The arms, being the thin lanky members, are, like the legs, commonly represented by lines. The same thing is noticeable in the drawings of savages. They appear, in the front view of the figure, as more or less

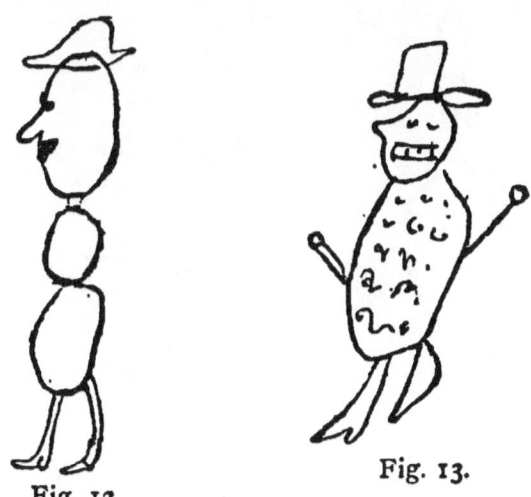

Fig. 12.   Fig. 13.

stretched out, so as to show beyond the trunk; and their appearance always gives a certain liveliness to the form, an air of joyous expression, as if to say, " Here I am !" (see Fig. 13, the drawing of a boy of six).

In respect of their structure a process of gradual evolution may be observed. The primal rigidity of the straight line yields later on to the freedom of an organ. Thus an attempt is made to represent by means of a curve the look of the bent arm, as in the accompanying drawing by a boy of five (Fig. 14). In other cases the angle of the elbow is indicated. This last improvement seems to come comparatively late in children's drawings, which here, as in other respects, lag behind the crudest outline sketches of savages.

The mode of insertion or attachment of the arms is noteworthy. Where they are added to the trunkless figure they sometimes appear as emerging from

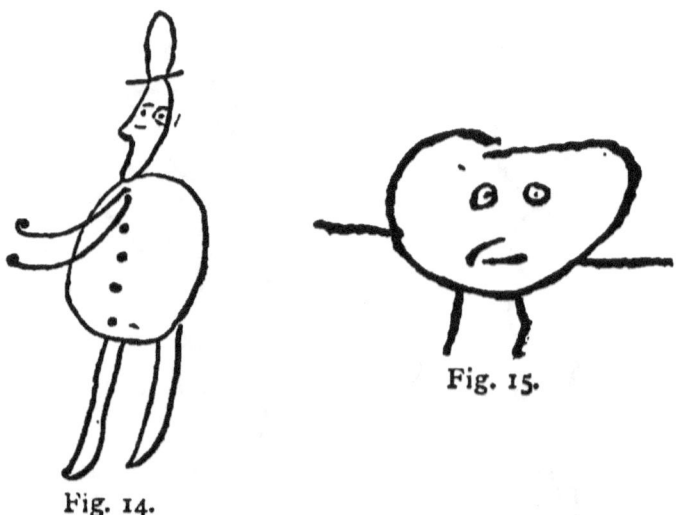

Fig. 15.

Fig. 14.

the sides of the head, as in a drawing by a boy of two and a half years (see Fig. 15), but more commonly, from the point of junction of the head and legs (see above, Fig. 7 (*b*)). After the trunk is added they appear to sprout from almost any point of this. It may be added that their length is often grotesquely exaggerated.

The arm in these childish drawings early develops the interesting adjunct of a hand. Like other features

this is apt at first to be amusingly forced into prominence by its size.

The treatment of the hand illustrates in a curious
way the process of artistic evolution, the movement
from a bare symbolic indication towards a more life-
like representation. Thus one of the earliest and
rudest devices I have met with, though in a few cases
only, is that of drawing strokes across the line of the
arm to serve as signs of fingers (Fig. 16).

It is an important advance when the branching lines

Fig. 16.—Humpty
Dumpty on the wall.

Fig. 17.

are set in a bunch-like arrangement at the extremity
of the arm-line. From this point the transition is
easy to the common "toasting-fork" arrangement,
in which the finger-lines are set on a hand-line (see
above, Figs. 8 and 7 (*b*)). From this stage, again,
there is but a step to the first crude attempt to give
contour first to the hand alone, as in Fig. 13, and
then to hand and fingers, as in Figs. 11 and 17.

Various odd arrangements appear in the first attempts to outline arm and hand. In one, which occurs

not infrequently, a thickened arm is made to expand
 into something like a fan-shaped
hand, as in Fig. 18.

There is a corresponding development of the foot from a
bare indication by a line to
something like a form in which
toes are commonly represented
by much the same devices as
fingers. In the better drawings,
however, one notes signs of a
tendency to hide the toes, and to indicate the notch
between the heel and the sole of the boot.

Fig. 18.

Side Views of Things.

So far, I have dealt only with the child's treatment
of the front view of the human face and figure. New
and highly curious characteristics begin to appear when
he attempts to give the profile aspect.

A child, it must be remembered, prefers the full face
arrangement, as he wants to indicate all its important
features, especially the two eyes. " If," writes a
Kindergarten teacher, " one makes drawings in profile
for quite little children, they will not be satisfied un-
less they see two eyes ; and sometimes they turn a
picture round to see the other side." This reminds
one of a story told, I believe, by Catlin of the Indian
chief, who was so angry at a representation of himself
in profile that the unfortunate artist went in fear of
his life.

At the same time children do not rest content with
this front view. After a time they try, without any aid

from the teacher, to grope their way to a new mode of representing the face and figure, which, though it would be an error to call it a profile drawing, has some of its characteristics.

The first clear indication of an attempt to give the profile aspect of the face is the introduction of the side view of the nose into the contour. The little observer is soon impressed by the characteristic, well-marked outline of the nose in profile; and the motive to bring this in is strengthened by his inability, already illustrated, to make much of the front view of the organ. The addition is made either by adding a spindle-like projection after completing the circle of the head, as in Figs. 6 and 7 (*a*), or more adroitly by modifying the circular outline. The other features, the eyes and the mouth, are given in full view as before.

It may well seem a puzzle to us how a normal child of five or six can complacently set down this self-contradictory scheme of a human head. How little any idea of consistency troubles the young draughtsman is seen in the fact that he will, not infrequently, reach the absurdity of doubling the nose, retaining the vertical line which did duty in the first front view along with the added nasal projection (see Fig. 19).

This appearance of the nose as a lateral projection is apt to be followed by a similar side view of the ear (as seen in Fig. 19), of the beard and other adjuncts which the little artist wants to display in the most advantageous way.

Some children stop at this mixed scheme, continuing to give the two eyes and the mouth, as in the front view, and frequently also the front view of the

13

body. This becomes a fixed conventional way of representing a man. With children of finer perception the transition to a correct profile view may be carried much further. Yet a lingering fondness for the two eyes is apt to appear at a later stage in this development of a consistent treatment of the profile; a feeling that the second eye is not in its right place prompting the artist in some cases to place it *outside the face* (see Fig. 20 (*a*) and (*b*)).

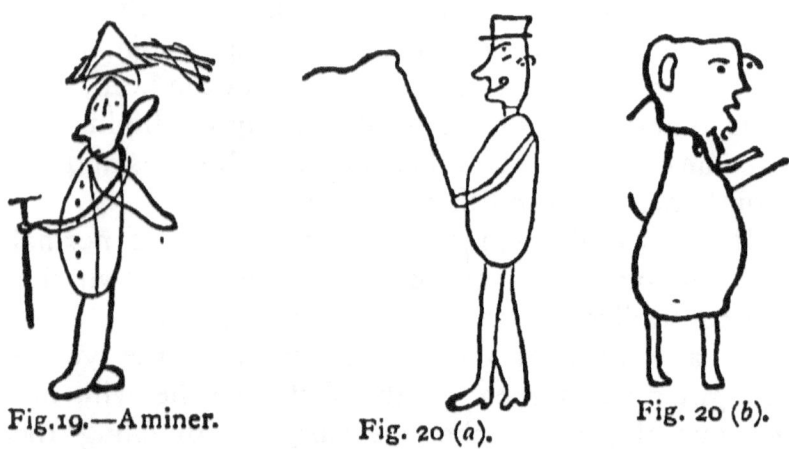

Fig.19.—A miner.   Fig. 20 (*a*).   Fig. 20 (*b*).

Other confusions are apt to appear in these early attempts at drawing a man in profile. The trunk, for example, is very frequently represented in front view with a row of buttons running down the middle, though the head and feet seem clearly shown in side view. The arms, too, not uncommonly are spread out from the two sides of the trunk just as in the front view.

It would take too long to offer a complete explanation of these characteristics of children's drawings.

I must content myself here with touching on one or two of the main causes at work.

First of all, then, it seems pretty evident that most children when they begin to draw are not thinking of setting down a likeness of what they see when they look at an object. In the first simple stage we have little more than a jotting down of a number of linear notes, a kind of rude and fragmentary description in lines rather than in words. Here a child aims at bringing into his scheme what seems to him to have most interest and importance, such as the features of the face, the two legs, and so forth. In the later and more ambitious attempt to draw a man in profile the old impulse to set down what seems important continues to show itself. Although the little draughtsman has decided to give to the nose, to the ear, and possibly to the manly beard and the equally manly pipe, the advantage of a side view, he goes on exhibiting those sovereign members, the two round eyes, and the mouth with its flash of serried teeth, in their full front-view glory. It is enough for him to know that the lord of creation has these members, and he does not trouble about so small a matter as our capability of seeing them all at the same moment.* In like manner a child will sometimes, on first clothing the human form, exhibit arms and legs through their covering (see Fig. 21 (*a*) and (*b*)). All this shows that even at this later and decidedly "knowing" stage of his craft he is not much nearer the point of view of our pictorial art than he was in the earlier stage of bald symbolism.

Much the same kind of thing shows itself in a child's manner of treating the forms of animals, which his pencil is wont to attack soon after that of man.

Here the desire to exhibit what is characteristic and worthy naturally leads at the outset to a representation of the body in profile. A horse is rather a poor affair looked at from the front. A child must show his four legs, as well as his neck and his tail. But though the profile seems to be the aspect selected, the little penciller by no means confines himself to a strict record of this. The four legs have to be shown

Fig. 21 (*a*) (from General Pitt Rivers' collection of drawings).

Fig. 21 (*b*) (reproduced from a drawing published by Mr. H.T. Lukens).

not half hidden by overlappings but standing quite clear one of another. The head, too, must be turned towards the spectator, or at least given in a mixed scheme—half front view, half side view (see Fig. 22 (*a*) and (*b*)).

A like tendency to get behind the momentary appearance of an object and to present to view what the child *knows* to be there is seen in early drawings of men on horseback, in boats, railway carriages,

houses, and so forth. Here the interest in the human
form sets at defiance the limitations of perspective,
and shows us the rider's second leg through the
horse's body, the rower's body through the boat,
and so forth.

The widespread appearance of these tendencies
among children of different European countries, of
half-civilised peoples, like the Jamaica blacks, as well
as among adult savages, shows how deeply rooted in
the natural mind is this quaint notion of drawing.

At the same time there are, as I have allowed, im-

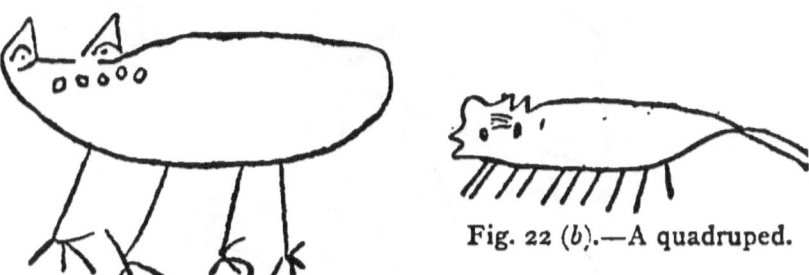

Fig. 22 (a).—A horse.

Fig. 22 (b).—A quadruped.

portant differences in children's drawings. A few
have the eye and the artistic impulse needed for
picturing, roughly at least, the *look* of an object. I
have lately looked through the drawings of a little
girl in a cultured home where every precaution was
taken to shut out the influences of example and
educational guidance. When at the age of four
years eight months she first drew the profile of the
human face she quite correctly put in only one eye,
and added a shaded projection for nose (see Fig. 23).
In like manner she was from the first careful to show
only one leg of the rider, one rein over the horse's

neck, and so forth; and would sometimes, with a
child's sweet thoughtfulness, explain to her mother
why she proceeded in this way.   Yet even in the case
of this child one could observe now and again a
rudiment of the tendency to bring in what is hidden.
Thus in one drawing she shows the rider's near leg
through the trouser; in another she introduces the
front view of a horse's nostrils (if not also of the ears)

Fig. 23.

in what is otherwise a drawing of the profile (see
Fig. 24 (*a*) and (*b*)).

   Yet while children's drawings are thus so far away
from those reproductions of the look of a thing which
we call pictures, they are after all a kind of rude
art.   Even the amusing errors which they contain,
though a shock to our notions of pictorial semblance,
have at least this point of analogy to art, that they
aim at selecting and presenting what is characteristic

and valuable. In many of the rude drawings with which we have here been occupied we may detect faint traces of individual originality, especially in the endeavour to give life and expression to the form. To this it is right to add that some drawings of young children from two to six which I have seen are striking proofs of the early development now and again of the artist's feeling for what is characteristic

Fig. 24 (*a*).

in line, and for the economic suggestiveness of a bare stroke (see Fig. 25 (*a*) and (*b*)). When once a child's eye is focussed for the prettiness of things the dawn of æsthetic perception is pretty sure to bring with it a more serious effort to reproduce their look. Among children, as among adults, it is love which makes the artist.

Fig. 24 (b).

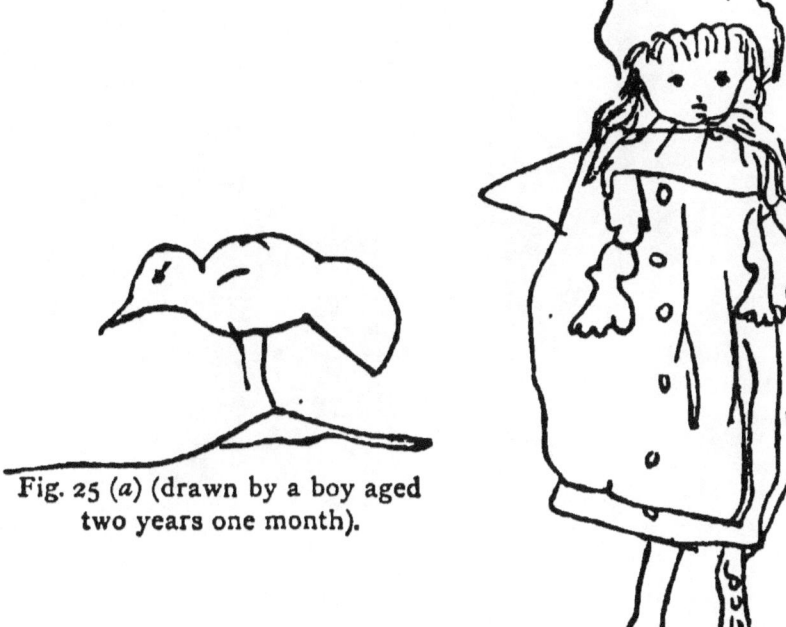

Fig. 25 (*a*) (drawn by a boy aged
two years one month).

Fig. 25 (*b*) (drawn by a girl of
five and a half years).

MISCELLANEOUS WORKS OF HERBERT SPENCER.

SOCIAL STATICS. New and revised edition, including "The Man *versus* The State," a series of essays on political tendencies heretofore published separately. 12mo. 420 pages. Cloth, $2.00.

CONTENTS.—Happiness as an Immediate Aim.—Unguided Expediency.—The Moral-Sense Doctrine.—What is Morality ?—The Evanescence [? Diminution] of Evil. —Greatest Happiness must be sought indirectly.—Derivation of a First Principle.— Secondary Derivation of a First Principle.—First Principle.—Application of the First Principle.—The Right of Property.—Socialism.—The Right of Property in Ideas.— The Rights of Women.—The Rights of Children.—Political Rights.—The Constitution of the State.—The Duty of the State.—The Limit of State-Duty.—The Regulation of Commerce.—Religious Establishments.—Poor-Laws.—National Education.—Government Colonization.—Sanitary Supervision.—Currency, Postal Arrangements, etc.— General Considerations.—The New Toryism.—The Coming Slavery.—The Sins of Legislators.—The Great Political Superstition.

"Mr. Spencer has thoroughly studied the issues which are behind the social and political life of our own time, not exactly those issues which are discussed in Parliament or in Congress, but the principles of all modern government, which are slowly changing in response to the broader industrial and general development of human experience. One will obtain no suggestions out of this book for guiding a political party or carrying a point in economics, but he will find the principles of sociology, as they pertain to the whole of life, better stated in these pages than he can find them expressed anywhere else. It is in this sense that this work is important and fresh and vitalizing. It goes constantly to the foundation of things."—*Boston Herald.*

EDUCATION : Intellectual, Moral, and Physical. 12mo. Paper, 50 cents ; cloth, $1.25.

CONTENTS: What Knowledge is of most Worth ?—Intellectual Education.—Moral Education.—Physical Education.

THE STUDY OF SOCIOLOGY. The fifth volume in the International Scientific Series. 12mo. Cloth, $1.50.

CONTENTS: Our Need of it.—Is there a Social Science?—Nature of the Social Science.—Difficulties of the Social Science.—Objective Difficulties.—Subjective Difficulties, Intellectual.—Subjective Difficulties, Emotional.—The Educational Bias.—The Bias of Patriotism.—The Class-Bias.—The Political Bias.—The Theological Bias.— Discipline.—Preparation in Biology.—Preparation in Psychology.—Conclusion.

THE INADEQUACY OF "NATURAL SELECTION." 12mo. Paper, 30 cents.

This essay, in which Prof. Weismann's theories are criticised, is reprinted from the *Contemporary Review*, and comprises a forcible presentation of Mr. Spencer's views upon the general subject indicated in the title.

New York: D. APPLETON & CO., 72 Fifth Avenue.

D. APPLETON & CO.'S PUBLICATIONS.

NEW EDITION OF SPENCER'S ESSAYS.

*E*SSAYS: *Scientific, Political, and Speculative.* By HERBERT SPENCER. A new edition, uniform with Mr. Spencer's other works, including Seven New Essays. Three volumes, 12mo, 1,460 pages, with full Subject-Index of twenty-four pages. Cloth, $6.00,

CONTENTS OF VOLUME I.

The Development Hypothesis.
Progress: its Law and Cause.
Transcendental Physiology.
The Nebular Hypothesis.
Illogical Geology.
Bain on the Emotions and the Will.

The Social Organism.
The Origin of Animal Worship.
Morals and Moral Sentiments.
The Comparative Psychology of Man.
Mr. Martineau on Evolution.
The Factors of Organic Evolution.*

CONTENTS OF VOLUME II.

The Genesis of Science.
The Classification of the Sciences.
Reasons for dissenting from the Philosophy of M. Comte.
On Laws in General, and the Order of their Discovery.
The Valuation of Evidence.
What is Electricity?
Mill *versus* Hamilton—The Test of Truth.

Replies to Criticisms.
Prof. Green's Explanations.
The Philosophy of Style.†
Use and Beauty.
The Sources of Architectural Types.
Gracefulness.
Personal Beauty.
The Origin and Function of Music.
The Physiology of Laughter.

CONTENTS OF VOLUME III.

Manners and Fashion.
Railway Morals and Railway Policy.
The Morals of Trade.
Prison-Ethics.
The Ethics of Kant.
Absolute Political Ethics.
Over-Legislation.
Representative Government— What is it good for?

State-Tampering with Money and Banks
Parliamentary Reform: the Dangers and the Safeguards.
"The Collective Wisdom."
Political Fetichism.
Specialized Administration.
From Freedom to Bondage.
The Americans.‡
Index.

* Also published separately. 12mo. Cloth, 75 cents.
† Also published separately. 12mo. Cloth, 50 cents.
‡ Also published separately. 12mo. Paper, 10 cents.

New York: D. APPLETON & CO., 72 Fifth Avenue.

*T*HE CARE AND FEEDING OF CHILDREN. *A Catechism for the Use of Mothers and Children's Nurses.* By L. EMMETT HOLT, M. D., Professor of Diseases of Children in the New York Polyclinic, Attending Physician to the Babies' Hospital, etc. 12mo. Cloth, 50 cents.

" The style of the Catechism is clear and simple, and it is the result of a long and successful practice of an eminent physician in every line pertaining to the health and management of children. This little work can not be too highly commended."—*Boston Home Journal.*

"The information contained in it is in the catechism form, and is particularly lucid in everything. An index makes it easy to turn to whatever is wanted, and the work, though small, bears the impress of careful thought as well as of authority."—*Chicago Times.*

*T*HE MOTHER'S MANUAL OF CHILDREN'S DISEASES. By CHARLES WEST, M. D., of the Royal College of Physicians, London. 12mo. Cloth, $1.25.

" The title fully explains its character, and it is only necessary to say that it is comprehensive, thorough, and learned, and fully adapted, in the character of its contents and its simple, direct style, to the wants of all households where there are 'children."—*Boston Post.*

"Dr. West is specially qualified to write on this subject. He was the founder of, and formerly physician to, the hospital for sick children in London, and has made their sufferings the study of his life."—*N. Y. Journal of Commerce.*

*T*HE MANAGEMENT OF INFANCY, *Physiological and Moral.* Intended chiefly for the Use of Parents. By ANDREW COMBE, M. D. Revised and edited by Sir JAMES CLARK, K. C. B., M. D., F. R. S., Physician to the Queen. First American from the tenth London edition. 12mo. Cloth, $1.50.

This valuable treatise embraces a most comprehensive plan, the author's aim being to avoid all *descriptions* of disease, and to found his precepts at every possible point on well-ascertained physiological principles.

*H*YGIENE FOR CHILDHOOD. Suggestions for the Care of Children after the Period of Infancy to Completion of Puberty. By FRANCIS H. RANKIN, M. D., President of the Newport Medical Society. 12mo. Cloth, 75 cents.

"The subject is one of universal importance, and Dr. Rankin has given it such an examination as can not fail to benefit his readers."—*Philadelphia Ledger.*

"A thoughtfully prepared manual, giving concisely the results of extensive practical experience, and is manifestly the work of one with whom it was a conscientious labor of love. The instruction it imparts is given in clear and simple language, and no point of essential importance regarding the health of children is passed by without full consideration."—*Boston Saturday Evening Gazette.*

*T*HE FARMER'S BOY. By CLIFTON JOHNSON, author of " The Country School in New England," etc. With 64 Illustrations by the Author. 8vo. Cloth, $2.50.

"One of the handsomest and most elaborate juvenile works lately published."— *Philadelphia Item.*

" Mr. Johnson's style is almost rhythmical, and one lays down the book with the sensation of having read a poem and that saddest of all longings, the longing for vanished youth."—*Boston Commercial Bulletin.*

" As a triumph of the realistic photographer's art it deserves warm praise quite aside from its worth as a sterling book on the subjects its title indicates. . . . It is a most praiseworthy book, and the more such that are published the better."—*New York Mail and Express.*

" The hook is beautiful and amusing, well studied, well written, redolent of the wood, the field, and the stream, and full of those delightful reminders of a boy's country home which touch the heart."—*New York Independent.*

"One of the finest books of the kind that have ever been put out."—*Cleveland World.*

" A book on whose pages many a gray-haired man would dwell with retrospective enjoyment."—*St. Paul Pioneer Press.*

" The illustrations are admirable, and the book will appeal to every one who has had a taste of life on a New England farm."—*Boston Transcript.*

*T*HE COUNTRY SCHOOL IN NEW ENG- LAND. By CLIFTON JOHNSON. With 60 Illustrations from Photographs and Drawings made by the Author. Square 8vo. Cloth, gilt edges, $2.50.

" An admirable undertaking, carried out in an admirable way. . . . Mr. Johnson's descriptions are vivid and lifelike and are full of humor, and the illustrations, mostly after photographs, give a solid effect of realism to the whole work, and are superbly reproduced. . . . The definitions at the close of this volume are very, very funny, and yet they are not stupid; they are usually the result of deficient logic."—*Boston Beacon.*

" A charmingly written account of the rural schools in this section of the country. It speaks of the old-fashioned school days of the early quarter of this century, of the mid-century schools, of the country school of to-day, and of how scholars think and write. The style is animated and picturesque. . . . It is handsomely printed, and is interesting from its pretty cover to its very last page."—*Boston Saturday Evening Gazette.*

" A unique piece of book-making that deserves to be popular. . . . Prettily and serviceably bound, and well illustrated."—*The Churchman.*

" The readers who turn the leaves of this handsome book will unite in saying the author has 'been there.' It is no fancy sketch, but text and illustrations are both a reality."—*Chicago Inter-Ocean.*

" No one who is familiar with the little red schoolhouse can look at these pictures and read these chapters without having the mind recall the boyhood experiences, and the memory is pretty sure to be a pleasant one."—*Chicago Times.*

" A superbly prepared volume, which by its reading matter and its beautiful illustra- tions, so natural and finished, pleasantly and profitably recalls memories and associations connected with the very foundations of our national greatness."—*N. Y. Observer.*

New York: D. APPLETON & CO., 72 Fifth Avenue.

PAUL AND VIRGINIA. By BERNARDIN DE SAINT-PIERRE. With a Biographical Sketch, and numerous Illustrations by Maurice Leloir. 8vo. Cloth, gilt top, uniform with " Picciola," " The Story of Colette," and " An Attic Philosopher in Paris." $1.50.

It is believed that this standard edition of " Paul and Virginia " with Leloir's charming illustrations will prove a most acceptable addition to the series of illustrated foreign classics in which D. Appleton & Co. have published " The Story of Colette," " An Attic Philosopher in Paris, and " Picciola." No more sympathetic illustrator than Leloir could be found, and his treatment of this masterpiece of French literature invests it with a peculiar value.

PICCIOLA. By X. B. SAINTINE. With 130 Illustrations by J. F. GUELDRY. 8vo. Cloth, gilt top, $1.50.

" Saintine's ' Picciola,' the pathetic tale of the prisoner who raised a flower between the cracks of the flagging of his dungeon, has passed definitely into the list of classic books. . . . It has never been more beautifully housed than in this edition, with its fine typography, binding, and sympathetic illustrations."—*Philadelphia Telegraph.*

" The binding is both unique and tasteful, and the book commends itself strongly as one that should meet with general favor in the season of gift-making."—*Boston Saturday Evening Gazette.*

" Most beautiful in its clear type, cream-laid paper, many attractive illustrations, and holiday binding."—*New York Observer.*

AN ATTIC PHILOSOPHER IN PARIS; or, A Peep at the World from a Garret. Being the Journal of a Happy Man. By ÉMILE SOUVESTRE. With numerous Illustrations. 8vo. Cloth, gilt top, $1.50.

" A suitable holiday gift for a friend who appreciates refined literature."—*Boston Times.*

" The influence of the book is wholly good. The volume is a particularly handsome one."—*Philadelphia Telegraph.*

" It is a classic. It has found an appropriate reliquary. Faithfully translated, charmingly illustrated by Jean Claude with full-page pictures, vignettes in the text, and head and tail pieces, printed in graceful type on handsome paper, and bound with an art worthy of Matthews, in half-cloth, ornamented on the cover, it is an exemplary book, fit to be ' a treasure for aye.' "—*New York Times.*

THE STORY OF COLETTE. A new large-paper edition. With 36 Illustrations. 8vo. Cloth, gilt top, $1.50.

" One of the handsomest of the books of fiction for the holiday season."—*Philadelphia Bulletin.*

" One of the gems of the season. . . . It is the story of the life of young womanhood in France, dramatically told, with the light and shade and coloring of the genuine artist, and is utterly free from that which mars too many French novels. In its literary finish it is well-nigh perfect, indicating the hand of the master."—*Boston Traveller.*

www.ingramcontent.com/pod-product-compliance
Lightning Source LLC
Chambersburg PA
CBHW020620030726

47497CB00007B/2344